THE MAESTRO O]

CW00868349

We are reunited with the loveable cast of characters that we met in Drew Launay's first novel about the sleepy Spanish village of Almijara, a place he describes as 'a cluster of birds nests stuck perilously to the steep slopes of the mountains'.

From the pompous school teacher Maestro Muñoz, the village's self-appointed intellectual, to canny Placido, owner of the Bar Alhambra, whose wife Conchita always nags him 'whenever she has the chance', we return to the Andalucía a few years after the death of General Franco, when telephones and electricity are still a marvel, and where every doorway is open to every neighbour and passerby, (after all, that *is* still the best way to find out all the gossip).

Who was the rich stranger staying at the Bar Alhambra? Why did he want to buy the barren and unprofitable olive groves? The dusty streets of the Spanish village of Almijara are buzzing with fevered speculation.

As insignificant an event as the arrival of an *extranjero* is big news in tiny, secluded Almijara. Imagine the hullaballoo caused by a whole film crew with lights, cameras and lots of money, who swarmed in one day.

But despite such upsets, the villagers simply drink, laugh, relax and life continues much as it has for centuries.

A

Book

THE MAESTRO OF ALMIJARA

Drew Launay

Illustrations by Melissa Launay

Published by Lewis-Fry Publications

Also by Drew Launay, published by
Lewis-Fry Publications

THE OLIVE GROVES OF ALMIJARA
(Available on Kindle and in print)

Foreword

by Melissa Launay

"This book was inspired by the kindness and eccentricity of the people of Frigiliana in southern Spain…"

My father, who sadly passed away in May 2013, was an author, playwright, humourist and broadcaster, writing under his real name, André Launay, but also Drew Launay, Andrew Laurance and Drew Lamark. He was fascinated by the Spanish way of life and its warm people, having moved to Andalucia in 1969 with his wife Eve and my two older brothers, Nick and Matthew. They were only the second foreign family to move to the sleepy town of Frigiliana at a time when Franco still ruled Spain. He was absorbed by the way of life, particularly in contrast to the hectic pace of the city he had left behind in London. He began writing short stories and diary entries based on the people he knew in Frigiliana and this book is partly based on his research and gathering of local tales during this time.

Having separated from Eve, he met my mother, 'a fiery, foot stamping, mad-as-a-sombrero, restless Andalucian scamp', to use his own words, and he published this book under her name, Maria Isabel Martin Rodriguez. She also helped him with the research, adding her own anecdotes and aiding him in compiling the following story.

The Maestro of Almijara is a revised version from the original 'The Maestro of Alhora', a sequel to 'The Olive Groves of Alhora', now available as The Olive Groves of Almijara. I hope you enjoy it as much as I do. Alhora doesn't exist as a town. All the anecdotes were inspired by true events that happened in Frigiliana during the 1970's under Franco's rule. It's a snapshot of an otherwise fairly undocumented period of time in a wonderful part of Spain, and a testimony not only to the aesthetic beauty and meditative, drowsy atmosphere of Frigiliana but also the hospitable spirit, kindness and eccentricity of its people.

Published by Lewis-Fry Publications

ISBN-13: 978-1537472584
ISBN-10: 1537472585

Chapter 1

The cemetery of Almijara was one and a half kilometres from the centre of the pueblo, or exactly one thousand, three hundred and seventy-two paces from the bar of the Alhambra Cafe.

Placido knew this for a fact because he had counted the steps himself many times during the forty-six funeral processions he had attended, and it had been confirmed by Ignacio, the carpenter, who had always been called on to act as judge in the settlement of bets on such important matters.

The decision, he remembered, had been a tricky one because it all depended on what a 'pace' was, but everyone had agreed, eventually, that a pace was the distance between the front foot and the back foot when walking behind the coffin in the funeral procession, and not one of Miguel's long strides when leading his mule back from the campo to go to the Alhambra.

Both Ignacio and Miguel were dead now, lying at rest somewhere within those beehive walls of morbid niches.

Placido looked around.

There were metal crucifixes, plastic virgins, multi-coloured rosaries and silver-framed photographs among the fresh and faded flowers, there were carved names, engraved names, printed names and hand-written names. Identity obviously followed one into the next life.

Conchita, holding an unnecessarily generous bunch of white chrysanthemums, pulled at his sleeve and led him to Don Enrique's tomb.

They had come to play homage to Don Enrique's memory.

'He left us the Alhambra and the olive groves, Placido. The least we can do is to remember the anniversary of his death.'

Nobody else had bothered; there weren't even any dead flowers on the old miser's monument, a tabernacle of marble covered with the names of the Velasco-Torres family, lest one should forget.

'He left them to you, not to me,' Placido had protested.

'He left you six hundred thousand pesetas.'

This was true, but he came dutifully to the cemetery often enough without having to be dragged up here first thing on a Monday morning.

Rolling a cigarette, he watched Conchita take an empty soup tin from someone else's grave, fill it with water from the little tap by the entrance gates, arrange the chrysanthemums neatly and place them on the tomb. It made it look even more desolate than before.

'*Buena*,' she said, apparently satisfied, making the sign of the cross. 'Now he cannot reproach me for being ungrateful.'

Placido lit his cigarette, allowed her to take his arm and thankfully started down the steps towards the pueblo.

'It's there again!' Conchita said looking down the road towards Orjena del Mar.

And it was! A large silver car, parked on the rise just above the very olive groves Conchita had inherited from Don Enrique.

In among the peaceful trees, a tall man with a balding head of white hair was walking around as though looking for something.

'Who is he?'

'A foreigner,' Placido said.

'What does he want?'

Placido shrugged his shoulders. It was a bit annoying not knowing, but he'd find out; someone in the bar would tell him.

'It's the fourth time he's been there.' Conchita protested.

When they got back to the Alhambra and Placido was checking the float in his cash register, Alfredo roared to a stop outside the door in his huge lorry and started to unload the week's supply of Cruz Campo beer.

'He's back again,' Alfredo said.

'We know,' Placido answered, a little sharply. It was beginning to irritate him now. In fact everything about the olive groves was beginning to irritate him. Because Conchita's land was on the way up to the village everyone who passed it felt it necessary to tell him what was going on there. And it was surprising what did go on - dogs mating, goats eating, lovers meeting by moonlight, strangers picking the olives. Between the wretched groves and Gonzales, the mayor, who left him in charge of all the pueblo business, he had no time to himself.

He'd had to suffer Gonzales for six months. Six months! Until he had hit on the idea of diverting Gonzales's interest from the welfare of the pueblo to his forgotten loved one in up in the north of Spain somewhere, Gonzales had nearly driven him to drink. not only had he turned out to be a tedious brother-in-law but a political pain in the neck as well.

And before Gonzales it had been Don Enrique.

'You are weak, Placido,' Conchita had always told him. 'Always doing Don

8

Enrique's bidding and getting nothing for it.'

When the old man had died and the pueblo had been without a titular head there had come the crazy elections for a Mayor, and Gonzales had been voted in.

'You are a fool, Placido,' Conchita had said knowledgeably. 'You let others walk over you, others use you, Gonzales will be another.'

And certainly for the first six months, the last six months, she had been proved right. Gonzales hadn't left him alone.

Gonzales in fact had proved to be quite unworthy of being Mayor of Almijara. He drank vast quantities of the bar's profits and was as hopeless as Placido at refusing to do things for other people. Conchita had been hopeless in refusing her long lost brother anything he asked for.

So they *were* richer. So they owned the Bar Alhambra, the olives groves and a car, but they didn't have to give *everything* away, they didn't have to be generous all the time.

It had become ridiculous and during the last six months they had too many quarrels, too many petty arguments over nothing. Finally, he had hit on the idea of mentioning the mythical Vincenta Turena de Lara Baron from Valadolid, whom Gonzales had supposedly lived with during the Civil War.

'Why don't you go up there and find out what has happened to her? If she married, she might now be a rich widow. If she did not marry she might have inherited a family fortune. If neither, she might still have that sparkle in her eyes which first made you desert the cause.'

Mentioning the word desertion had of course prompted a fearful quarrel. Gonzales had fiercely smashed his heavy fist down on the stainless-steel top of the bar and had fractured his hand. This had necessitated going down to Almijara to see the doctor who had pronounced it cracked, like its owner, and by the time he came back with his arm in a sling, Gonzales had sobered up completely.

If Placido had felt a little guilty at throwing the accusation, it had at least served as a reminder, pin-pointing their relationship. Placido knew the truth about the past, after which Gonzales had made less demands, given less orders and finally considered the idea of going up north to Valadolid to see his beloved Vincenta, and accepted money to help him on his way.

But so far he had not gone. Like a conquering general he had requisitioned and occupied the Velasco-Torres house next door, had stuck the national flag on the front balcony and called it his headquarters. No one, in fact had taken a blind bit of notice, which was perhaps why he spent most of his days alone in one of the empty bedrooms, drinking.

So it was, on this bright May morning, with the hot spring sun beating down on the narrow cobbled streets of Almijara, that Placido admitted that he only had himself to blame if another local burden was placed on his shoulders. To be honest, he preferred it this way. And so did others.

Nobody wanted a new cinema where old Jorge's granary stood, or an expensive new projector for the present cinema. Nobody wanted Gonzales to show 'Partido Socialista' propaganda films, or his boring lectures on Cuba. Where the fool totally failed as a politician was in not having anything more to fight against. Franco's death had taken the sting out of so many revolutionaries, especially the old ones, as that other old fool Muñoz had been quick to point out.

And how *that* man has changed! El Maestro, who lived in sin with that toothless hag Angustias. They at least seemed very happy about the arrangement despite El Cura excommunicating them both and forbidding them entry into his church, and vainly attempting to have Muñoz sacked as the village schoolmaster, for a replacement would have been hard to find.

At least behind the bar he was the master of his own empire. The spotlessness of his stainless-steel top with the two glass showcases in one of which he would place the tapas - chicken livers, *garbanzos, pimientos fritos, bocarones en vinagre, gambas*. In the other he put the doughnuts, *tortas*, cakes from Orjena del Mar. Behind him the line of bottles, the *vinos tintos, blancos*, the *terreno* wine, the cognacs, the *anis seco* and *dulce*; under the bar in the refrigerator, he kept the beer, the coca cola, the Fanta *limon* and *naranja*.

To the left, in the specially built alcove of white tiles and brick, was the Italian coffee machine, his first ever investment. What a fortune that had made him. Only twice had it gone wrong, over all these years, but only because he had looked after it. Manolo, his assistant, had looked after it too, if sometimes over-enthusiastically, banging his coffee dregs out of the screw in percolator cups.

It was while he was giving this machine its final morning polish, winking at his own reflection in the chrome panel above the steam taps, that the *extranjero* came in. Placido had never seen him close to, but an *extranjero* he certainly was to these parts.

'*Buenosh diash*,' the tall man said in pure Castellano.

'*Buenos dias*,' Placido answered. He was delighted of course, but determined not to show it. He wanted to rush upstairs and call Conchita, but that would never do.

From his shoes, his white trousers, the cut of this dark blue short-sleeved shirt with its unnecessary pockets, it was clear that the man was by no means poor. The gold watch round his left wrist alone was worth a few *duros*.

What would he order? a coffee with a brandy? A whisky or gin and tonic? A bottle of champagne? He had one down in the cellar which he could charge a bit more for now that it was two years older.

'A glass of *agua mineral*,' the man said. '*Con gaz*.'

There was more profit on that than a glass of wine, but it did not augur well.

Placido opened the bottle of mineral water, found a clean glass and poured the sparkling liquid into it.

He would not ask questions, the stranger would eventually give it all away. They always did.

The white-haired man sat down on one of the bar stools and dug into one of his pockets for a packet of cigarettes, producing a gold cigarette lighter to match the wrist watch. He had a pair of expensive looking sun glasses hanging out of another pocket.

Conchita came padding down from upstairs to prepare the tapas. She gave the man a nice smile, nearly too nice. There was no need to ingratiate oneself with the rich because they were rich.

'From Granada?' Placido asked, washing up a cup which did not need washing.

'Madrid,' the man said, and he offered Placido a cigarette, which was nice, and very acceptable. He even lit it for him with the expensive gold lighter.

'Holiday?'

'No I've come to purchase some land.'

Cochita was back again and nearly dropped the bowl of olives she had used as an excuse to come in.

'Land? Are you a farmer?' She asked.

Was he a farmer! He would know as much about farming as she would know about mending a television set.

'No. I want to build a villa.'

'Up here, in the village?' Conchita was not being too discreet.

'I like the village very much.'

'There's not much land around here for sale,' Conchita said pessimisti-

11

cally. 'Not near the road, or with good views.'

Placido was afraid she was being too obvious.

Would the stranger want to buy the olive groves? It would bring class to the village to have such an extranjero build a villa. The first maybe of a few, then of many? After all, Madrilenos had already acquired land down in Orjena and built themselves villas. So far no one had ventured this far up into the mountains.

'I suppose you know most people in the village?' The man asked.

'Everyone.'

'And the land they own?'

'Yes, and the land they own.'

'I'm particularly interested in the olive orchard that runs due west down the slope from the road out. The land rises then falls, the trees are very pretty there, and the view is splendid.'

'I know the place you mean.'

Conchita was standing looking at him with her mouth open. Only last week they had discussed what to do with all the land they had inherited and Conchita had wondered about selling it. But no one would want to buy such useless land unless they were going to cultivate the olive trees which were getting old.

'I could make enquiries for you.'

'That would be kind.'

'Where are you staying?'

'Down in Orjena.'

'The Parador?'

'No... one of the pensións.'

Maybe he wasn't too rich then. A man like that would normally stay at the Parador de Turismo. Why not if you could afford it?

Conchita's expression must have shown her surprise for the man explained, 'I don't like the conventional hotels. I am retired now and seek the simpler life. That is why I want to live up here.'

'You could stay here,' Conchita suggested. 'We have rooms.'

'I would like that. Do you have one with a view?'

'Not only do we have one with a view over the valley, but a view of the very olive groves you are interested in.'

'Show me,' the man said, and Conchita opened the door wide for him and led the way up the stairs.

Too curious to be able to stand behind the bar and wait, Placido followed them both to the first floor landing, down the passage to the end of the room.

Conchita always kept the room ready in case a traveller wanted to stay in Almijara, but the pueblo was on the way to nowhere at the end of the valley; beyond rose the high Sierras with its pine forests and granite peaks.

Placido stood in the doorway and watched as Conchita proudly patted the lace bed cover her mother had made, stroked the mahogany chest of drawers with its swivel mirror, inclined her head slightly at the huge crucifix, on the wall. She unlocked the shutters and threw them open. The morning sun blazed in, and she stepped aside to allow the man to have a look.

The small balcony was hardly wide enough to stand on, but it enabled a person to learn out and have a good look up and down the valley. The olive groves were below on the left, on the slopes opposite Emilio's vineyard, and in the far, far distance was the sea. So many visitors to Almijara suggested that he should open up the southern side of the Bar Alhambra so that they could sit and look at the view, but they didn't realise the cost. And who of the villagers would want to sit in the sun and gaze at the land they worked all day? All they wanted to do was stay indoors in the cool and play dominoes or watch television.

'It smells a little musty,' Conchita said. 'We don't have many guests. The last one was Paquita's uncle. Do you remember, Placido?'

He remembered.

'I'd like to have the room for a day or two,' the extranjero said. 'Is one permitted to park the car in the village?'

'It is permitted, but not too wise,' Placido said, leading the way down the stairs. 'The streets are very narrow and early in the morning old Bautista takes his herd of goats through, and the mules use it to go to the campo.'

'Will it be safe just outside the Guardia Civil?'

'If it isn't safe there, it won't be safe anywhere. Sargento Javier will keep an eye on it.'

'I'll park it there and return with my bags.'

And he left without paying for the mineral water, which made Placido wonder for a moment whether he was rich because he never paid for anything, or whether as a resident he now expected everything to go on the bill.

What was happening to the world outside if rich men now wanted to retire to such backwaters as this? It was the ambition of everyone in the village to get out, not come in, get out and make their fortune... like Paquita's uncle,

Fernando.

It had never been known exactly who Fernando's father was, a passing gypsy perhaps, but his mother had all the pride of Andalucía in her blood and she had brought up Fernando, her only son, to be a gentleman. Her family had come from Sevilla and the *majo* tradition of glittering velvets and filigree buttons, tags and tassels, dressing as brightly as the sun, external appearances being all, had been deeply instilled in him as a boy.

He was the *majo* of Almijara, their only one, and of course at fifteen years old, just before the outbreak of the Civil War, he had volunteered, had gone for a while, returned once in a glittering uniform which someone had unkindly said belonged to a circus, and then had gone again, never to be seen until his niece Paquita's wedding.

Two weeks before the boda rumour had it that Fernando would come back from Málaga where he was reported to be living in splendour, and on the festive day he had indeed appeared in a white Mercedes taxi with Málaga plates.

His suit had not been dazzling, but of a very distinguished *muy elegante* grey, a hat and a waistcoat of beads. He had carefully trimmed sideboards, a pencil thin moustache and his piercing brown eyes had sparkled and made Conchita blush.

He had brought everyone drinks in the bar, ordered champagne and insisted on paying for it immediately, as though no one would believe his wealth. His shoes, of black patent leather, had such style that even Placido had to admire them, along with his white cuffs and his grey silk cummerbund. He had impressed, had made his niece so proud, although Conchita had been a little disappointed when she took him up his black coffee and anis seco the morning after the wedding to see that he did not wear silk pyjamas; instead he wore a not-too-white vest, and possibly nothing else in bed.

He had been generous, handling Manolo a large *propina* and giving several *duros* to Pilar who came to help clear up. He had ordered a taxi from Orjena and all the family, if not half the village had waved him goodbye, sad that he might never be seen again, but happy that at least one of Almijara's children had become wealthy.

No one had managed to find out how he had become so rich; the kinder ones said that he was an extremely astute businessman, that he bred the best bulls in Spain; others that he had made a fortune during the Civil War supplying arms to both sides, or that he was a pimp and ran a brothel.

14

Then he, Placido, of all people, had found out the truth.

On a rare visit to Málaga, one of those bi-annual expeditions before Semana Santa when he went with Conchita to purchase supplies for the bar, he had stopped in the central gardens to use the public lavatory.

The urinals had been crowded, so he had slipped into one of the cubicles and immediately there had been a brutal banging on the door and an irate voice demanding payment.

'I'm only having a pee!' he had shouted.

'For a crap you must pay hombre!' the lavatory attendant had screamed.

Placido, furious, had opened the door while relieving himself and bawled indignantly, 'See for yourself, I am not sitting down, I am peeing!'

Then he had turned and found himself facing Fernando, Fernando the *fanfarrón*, Fernando the *majo*. He was wearing an old pair of trousers, and even older shirt and sandal; he was unshaven, a tramp.

'Hombre!' Placido had said, and Fernando had looked straight through him, deliberately failing to recognise him.

'Fernando, what are you doing here?'

Fernando had cleverly turned his head to look at whom Placido was talking, and smiled; then he put out his hand.

'The cubicle is two pesetas.'

Placido had smiled, done up his flies, dug deep into his trouser pocket and brought out a five peseta piece which he pressed into Fernando's hand.

Fernando had looked at it, dug deep into his pocket and brought out the change.

Placido had smiled, shaken his head and waved, telling him to keep the change. But Fernando's proud eyes had blazed and he had thrust the change back at Placido. It was the moment of truth.

Placido had taken it and smiled.

'Hombre, if you were anyone but Fernando you would have accepted it.'

'And if you were anyone else Placido, you would not consider it strange that one's pride is more important than a three peseta tip!'

Placido had turned on his heels and walked out into the tropical gardens.

He had mixed feelings about the encounter. Others might have felt pity for Fernando, but he had felt that the man was a survior whatever indignities or tragedies he had suffered in life he knew how to cope. Somehow he had managed to save enough for his niece's wedding to put up a show, it had been his day. Fernando probably knew more about life than the majority of people who used his urinals.

And he had never told anyone about the meeting, he had preserved the *majo*'s pride. Besides, it had not been that important.

What was important was whether the extranjero would come back and pay for the mineral water.

Chapter 2

In the first-floor school room, with its windows opening on to a long balcony overlooking the village square, El Maestro, Miguel Muñoz, picked his nose and faced his thirty-four children.

He was not aware that he was picking his nose; it was a bad habit he had got into when young and no one had bothered to correct it, except Angustias.

'*Malo, malo,*' the cheeky son of Ricardo the baker said out loud, slapping his own hand in front of his face.

The boy was having the temerity to copy Angustias. It had become public knowledge then that she slapped him, and he was being held to ridicule.

'*Niño,*' El Maestro said, looking over the top of his reading glasses, 'I will stop picking my nose if you can stand up and recite your seven times table.'

The boy stood up to the great glee of the rest of the class. He daringly stared straight at Muñoz and stammered out, 'Seven times one is six, seven times two is fifteen, seven times three is twenty-four...'

'Very funny,' Muñoz said pretending to stick two fingers up his nose, 'Now I promise to amuse you more if you recite your twelve times tables correctly. But if you don't you stay in after school until you can.'

The boy gulped, the school room became quiet and Muñoz glared down at all of them.

He knew how and when to command respect. He knew that he had become complicated and unmanageable since Angustias had moved in with him and they openly lived together; his character had changed: he could be funny, amusing, kind and generous one day, and very ugly the next.

When he was ugly, the children knew it was best not to make jokes about him, for he still had the power. He had failed to become mayor, it had not mattered much, but he had not failed to get a woman to look after him.

'Twelve ones are twelve, twelve twos are twenty-four, twelve threes are thirty-six...' Ricardo's son incanted.

He sailed through the tables with little difficulty, he was intelligent, which was why El Maestro allowed him a little licence. He allowed the children to do a lot more now because Angustias had made him more human.

She had such an infectious sense of humour, such a total disregard for the conventions he had upheld over the years that his life had to change. Her sense of humour was not so much crude as abysmally vulgar. Her life had been spent scrubbing other people's floors and, as she had explained, from that position all one did was to stare up other women's skirts or straight at men's *pitos* which put everyone on the same stupid level. That was her view of life and no one was going to convince her it was different.

At first, he had found it quite unbearable, but he had been caught by the oldest form of deception, she had got him into bed, had seen him undressed, knew him as no other woman in the world had known him, and therefore owned his soul.

She made no demands on him whatsoever except that he should try to see the reverse side of the coin to the life he had led. She had a sense of decorum at home, the dinner table was laid daily with a clean tablecloth; he was no longer allowed to be untidy; his shirts and two suits were scrupulously cleaned and pressed, his socks darned and his shoes polished so that the world had seen the difference and approved.

In exchange, she did not allow him to be serious about the things that were clearly not serious at all - El Cura, for instance - who went around with a smell under his nose because he was employed by God. No one was employed by God, no one had His ear more than others - if the God that El Cura preached about so much existed at all.

She was not an atheist, nor an agnostic, she believed in a power above all, even in a day of judgement, but she believed that the judges had a heart and a sense of humour. In her book, all those idiots who believed that lighting a candle to a saint did any good were mad, quite mad. There were quite a number of much better things to do with a candle, and her crudity, when she had first said this to Muñoz, had offended him; she had slapped him so hard on the back as she roared with vulgar laughter that he had choked on the slice of chorizo he was chewing, and that had sent her into more paroxysms of laughter.

She had totally annihilated his pomposity as a Maestro and of course had relentlessly told him what the village thought of him and what the children said of him.

His behaviour towards la Viuda Bendicion had been village history since the day he had exposed himself by mistake to Sagento Javier. Who was he to be pompous and to pretend arrogance? Anyway he couldn't allow himself to be arrogant, he did not have the figure for it. To be arrogant you had to be thin and tall and have a large nose. He was small and fat and had a bulbous nose. He had an imbiber's nose so he should drink more, and she had bought him a bottle of *terreno* wine and filled his glass up every night as they sat across the round table on a winter's night, gossiping about the village.

Angustias was one big laugh, and the biggest laugh of all was to come that evening when they sat down together with the window open looking out across the valley at the stars above and the mountains, and she said she had something funny to tell him. He had recharged his glass and lit one of his black *cigarillos* and settled back against the cushions she had specially made for him, and waited to hear the village gossip. She always came up with a good story, and this one was the best of all.

'I am pregnant,' she announced. 'You are going to be a *papa*, Maestro Miguel Muñoz. How's that for a laugh?'

The cold shiver that ran down his spine was quite simply that of fear. He recognised it. He had experienced it several times before, and it surprised him. But what, exactly, was he afraid of? The shame? What shame?

There was nothing shameful about making a woman pregnant at his age. He would have to marry her now, of course. Was that what had caused the spasm of fear? He was delighted, and she seemed happy enough. What then was the shiver for?

He looked across at her, her fat arms crossed over her already protruding stomach, her thick hips, that inane smile on her face, daring him to be displeased. He looked at her and smiled, and the smile broadened, became a grin and when she started laughing he started laughing too.

He got up, threw his arms around her as best he could, for they were both on the fat side and it was never easy to embrace, and they did a little dance.

'I thought you were taking that pill,' he said, remembering how silly he had thought her when she had told him she was taking precautions. 'At your age?' he had questioned. 'Is that necessary?' Then he had realised that taking the pill had made her feel younger, had made the affair even more youthful than it could ever possibly be.

'Yes, I took them,' Angustias said.

'And they did not work?'

'Obviously not.'

'Those pills are no good then.'

'A little bit my fault,' she explained. 'The doctor said I didn't take them the right way.'

'Which way should you have taken them?'

'In the mouth, with a glass of water every day.'

19

'And you didn't take one every day?'

'Yes. But I didn't put it in my mouth!'

She thought it all so funny that she collapsed in a heap of laughter on the chair. 'Where else would you take a pill to stop a baby? After all that's where it goes in and comes out! I thought... But it's just like an aspirin.'

Muñoz didn't think it funny, he thought it ridiculous. That was what was so incredible about Angustias, her total and incessant sense of the ridiculous. He would have to get used to it, used to the laughter behind his back, because this story would be around the village in a flash, if it wasn't general knowledge already.

And there was a knock on the door. It was Dolores of the Caramelos, who ran the little sweet kiosk in the square, with a plastic bag full of something soft.

'These belonged to my granddaughter. I knitted them myself.'

As she shook the bag upside down over the table, out fell a quantity of tiny little sweaters, bonnets, socks, all so small that Muñoz could not believe that someone had seriously knitted them for a human being. It would be that small when it arrived, it would be that small despite her size, his size.

'*Muchas gracias* Dolores,' Angustias said, and the two women hugged each other.

It was of course a victory for womanhood and would be regarded as such by all in the village. For anyone of her age to produce was curious enough, for a spinster to produce and thus force her man to marry her was unbelievable.

Dolores looked at Muñoz and wagged her finger at him. It was like being a child again. He had eaten a forbidden sweet, done something naughtier than that, but it didn't feel much different at the moment.

He felt very happy, aware that a whole new life wad going to open up in front of him. There would of course be problems. El Cura would have something to say about it, but nature had taken its course and he was going to make the women his bride: he would have to announce their proposed wedding very soon, in fact he would let his intentions be known right now to quell all possible criticism, and who better to tell than Placido? Where better to start the gossip than the Bar Alhambra?

As he left the house and crossed the square he already felt his footsteps becoming lighter, sprightlier. What would Placido say? Placido who was only six years younger than himself. Didn't such an event open up completely new vistas?

And he smiled at old Felipe and he smiled at even older Antonio, and he smiled at El Tonto, the village idiot, who was on his knees in the middle of the cobbled land desperately trying to pick up the white cross Manuel, the electrician had painted to mark the spot where a pole would one day be erected to carry an electric cable up to Leoncio's new house.

What if *his* heir grew up to be retarded like that? What guarantee was there that a child would be born intelligent? The thought sent another shiver down his back, justified this time: the fear of fathering a fool. At his age it could happen. He would consult the doctor. He would not talk about it to Angustias because she would only laugh at his concern, but he would consult the doctor. Maybe he should have given up smoking?

To be a father at his age! It would change him completely. He had the responsibility of so many other people's children all his life, so it should not be difficult to be responsible for his own. All his wisdom would now be passed on. And he had never thought of it.

For all those years that he had sat behind that desk gazing down at those young faces, imparting his knowledge, he had never once thought of himself as a father. *Un Padre!*

He would have to change all his ways. He would have to see El Cura. He didn't want the child born illegitimate. All those dreams he had of becoming a great man himself, a man of the village, a mayor, a benefactor, seeing his statue in the centre of the square, all those dreams could be passed on to his son, or daughter.

Did it matter? Hardly. He would prefer a son of course. He would prefer a son.

> *Un bello niño de junco,*
> *anchos hombros, fino talle,*
> *piel de nocturna manzana,*
> *boca triste y ojos grandes...*

(A handsome willowy lad, wide of shoulder, slender of waist, skin of nocturnal apple, sad mouth and large eyes... *San Gabriel*, Federico Garcia Lorca)

Boys, of course were called up and killed in wars. Maybe there would be no more wars.

What ambitions would he have for him. To be a great teacher like his father?

He was no great teacher. Fatherhood would allow him to be humble, he would accept his humility. He would now live for someone else.

But Angustias, that mad woman who had taken him by storm, how would he control her? Would he ever be allowed to enjoy his own seriousness again?

She had her irritating side. Her total disrespect for his work, for his noble thoughts. Yet she treated him as a woman should treat a man, but without ceremony. His breakfast was always ready when he got up before going to the classroom, his midday meal was already there punctually. On Sundays, she insisted he wore his blue suit, dusted now so that the years of cigarette ash on the lapels had vanished.

And she cared for his health. At the first sign of a sneeze out came the *manzanilla*. A twinge of the stomach and out came the bicarbonate.

At first, he had found it strange to have this large body next to him in bed. She snored, she smelt of onions all the time, but she had also brought into the house a number of other smells, feminine smells which had never before entered his bachelor kingdom. Bottles of shampoo and handcream had appeared on his chest of drawers, on the bathroom-shelf above the washbasin. She was not vain, she knew her looks had gone, but she looked after herself though two of her front teeth were missing. You could smell her cleanliness. She was much cleaner than him, and though he hated it now, took a shower every other day. The water was cold, but it was good for the health and he felt better for it.

Rosario, the butcher's wife, waved at him as he passed her door. Magdalena in among her vegetables smiled and waved. Had they always been so friendly?

He reached the Bar Alhambra, it was still early, so the place was empty; Conchita was mopping the floor. They were rich now, Placido and Conchita owned the place, but all that it had done for them it seemed, was make them work twice as hard. Gonzales, Placido's brother-in-law, had caused problems. Everyone knew that. He had not turned out to be such a good mayor with all his talk of reform and politics. The old cinema had become his temple. He showed films in there which bored the children, but little else.

Placido greeted him very warmly with a big broad smile; he even came out from behind the bar and hugged him and patted him on the cheek.

'*Felicidades, hombre!*'

So the village knew already.

'When are you going to make an honest woman of her?'

Before he could answer, Emilio came in with Alfredo, followed by Paco and Sebastian. They all took his hand and shook it warmly, smacked him on the back and offered him a drink.

Placido uncharacteristically brought out the cognac and filled all their glasses. He didn't want a cognac but a coffee, but they were drinking his health so he had to drink as well.

Paquita came in with Ricardo, and Rosario with Magdalena. The women drank *anis dulce* and suddenly it was quite a party.

'You want a *niño* or a *niña*?'

'A boy, *tonta*! What else would he want?'

'What will you call it?'

'Maybe it'll be twins.'

'Have you had twins in the family?'

'Are you sure you're the father?'

Already new ideas were being planted in his mind, things he had never thought about.

'You can have Manolito's cot if you want, he's outgrown it now.'

And then the noisy group of people suddenly fell silent as a tall white-haired man appeared in the doorway. Muñoz had never seen him before but knew immediately he was the *extranjero* who had visited the village several times.

'*Buenash tardesh,*' he said in pure Castellano.

It pleased Muñoz. It pleased his ear to hear such perfect diction.

They made way for the *extranjero* who went to sit quietly at a table by himself. He was a gentleman that one, a *majo*.

'A good day for walking,' Paco said to him.

What inanity! Every day was good for walking except when it was raining, and it hadn't rained now for two months.

Muñoz eased his way nearer the stranger's table and raised his glass to him.

'From Madrid?'

The man nodded.

'*Vacaciones?*'

'No I've come here to retire.'

'In this pueblo?'

The man nodded again.

Muñoz shrugged his shoulders. Everyone had a different set of values.

'You are not from these parts?' The *extranjero* said.

'Originally from Cataluña,' Muñoz answered.

'And how long have you been down here?'

'Many years,' Muñoz said. 'Many years.'

'He's going to be a father,' Paco butted in. 'He's sixty-three and he's going to be a father.'

'Congratulations,' said the extranjero kindly.

Muñoz felt a trifle irritated. He didn't want the whole world to know. Fatherhood was a private affair between him and Angustias and maybe God, no one else, but then, on the other hand, he could hear Angustias laughing at such a thought if he had expressed it out loud.

'Come and sit down, join me in a drink,' the extranjero said. 'My name is Anselmo.'

'Muñoz,' Muñoz said. 'Miguel Muñoz.'

And he shook the man's hand.

He was clinically clean, this man. His shirt was spotless, he had a gold wrist watch, a ring, long fingers, bright blue eyes. A man of distinction. A *Marqués* perhaps, an aristocrat certainly.

As Paco and Emilio left to take their mules on up to their houses and Rosario and Magdelana left to go back to their *tiendas*, Placido went down to the cellars for more wine and Muñoz was left alone with the *extranjero*.

'One has dreams most of one's life you know,' he said. 'You work in a city every day and escape maybe twice a year to the sea and the fresh air, and you dream that when you retire you will live in that fresh air always. That time has come, and I want to embrace the air of Andalucía and its people.' And staring into space the *extranjero* started to recite...

El campo
de olivos
se abre y se cierra
como un abanico.
Sobre el olivar
hay un cielo hundido
y una lluvia oscura
de luceros frios...

Muñoz's eyes widened. A man after his own heart. Could it be that this day would not only announce the arrival of an heir but the arrival in the village of a kindrid spirit, someone intelligent to whom he could talk, and talk about poetry, about books?

Muñoz finished the poem...

> *Tiembla junco y penumbra*
> *a la orilla del rio.*
> *Se riza el aire gris.*
> *Los olivos...*

(The field of the olive trees opens and shuts like a fan. Over the olive grove is a deep sky and dark rain of cold stars. By the river bank, reeds and darkness trembles.)

'You are a man of letters then?' The *extranjero* said.

'I am the village teacher.'

'I should have known.'

Muñoz sipped his fourth brandy. The last time he had drunk so much he had got into that embarrassing situation with the Sargento Javier.

'You know all the people in the village well, then?'

'I have taught all of those under the age of forty.'

'So you know their sense of values?'

Muñoz was not sure what he meant.

'Moral sense of value or money sense of values?' He asked. He was rusty on intellectual conversation, he was aware of it. He was also aware that it was hardly with Angustias that this would improve.

'I want to buy some land,' the *extranjero* said. 'I want to build myself a villa. Will that offend, do you think? A foreigner building himself a new house.'

Muñoz pursed his lips. The man was more sensitive to things than most other people.

'You see, I would buy an old house and convert it, but there are none outside the village. There is however an old cortijo that could be converted and added to.'

He had seen this in magazine articles, people from the cities purchasing old farmhouses and barns and converting them into habitable dwellings. Paco, Emilio and such would never understand, they would think the man mad. Even Placido would think him mad, and yet it would help the village.

This man was so obviously wealthy.

'You were in business?' He asked.

'No. I was a surgeon.'

A surgeon. This explained the white hands, the long well manicured fingers, the clinical appearance of the man. He knew more about him already than anyone else.

'You have seen a cortijo you want?'

'Indeed, the one on the bend of the road going down to Orjena de Mar. The one that belongs to Placido.'

So, Placido would gain again.

'I would need a good builder.'

'Have you started negotiating with Placido?'

'No. I don't even know if he wants to sell.'

'Would you like me to enquire for you?'

'Indeed I would. And if there is anything I can do for you, any time.'

'You could answer me one question,' Muñoz said. 'You are a doctor after all. As you have heard, I am to be a father...'

'And you're worried about your age?'

'Yes.' This man was so intelligent.

'How is you wife? Healthy?'

'As strong as an ox. One of the hardiest women alive.'

'Then have no fears. It is not all that unusual.'

'Thank you doctor. I needed reassuring.' Then Muñoz added, wanting to give something back, 'You realise that, as we have no resident doctor in the pueblo, you will be called on continuously as soon as people hear you are a doctor.'

'Yes.'

'That will not be much of a retirement.'

'When you retire, Maestro, do you think that you will want to stop answering the questions asked by children hungry for knowledge?'

'No,' said Muñoz. And he felt so elated, so fortunate at having met a man whose intellect could match his own, that he ordered another cognac for Doctor Anselmo, and another one for himself.

Chapter 3

The negotiations for the *extranjero* to purchase Conchita's olive groves start-ed the following morning. Muñoz, having broached the subject with Placido, left it to both parties to sort themselves out.

In the back room of the Bar Alhambra the three sat around a table sipping strong coffee and got down to business.

The land Don Anselmo wanted would include the ruined cortijo, five acres around it, a right of way from the road, the *sequía*, and the water butt. His intention was to build a four bedroomed villa with a swimming pool looking south west, with a garage at road level if he could get planning permission from the local council, the *ayuntamiento*.

Placido knew that, agriculturally, the land had little to recommend it; the olive trees were so old their annual yield was not even worth picking. Nothing could have pleased him more than to sell it, but obviously the man would not buy unless he could build. The *ayuntamiento*, at present consisted of himself and Gonzales. Gonzales, he knew, would on principle oppose any building on the grounds that it would allow capitalist infiltration into the village. It would therefore require a great deal of diplomacy and subtlety to persuade Gonzales to allow a building, if indeed he was to be consulted at all.

If he was not there, if he was absent from the village at the time when the application was put in, then all Placido would have to do was hand over some sort of document to Don Anselmo giving him planning permission.

But how to get rid of Gonzales?

That afternoon, instead of their usual *siesta*, Placido and Conchita sat in the back room and discussed a way of dealing with the problem.

The idea Placido put forward was quite simple, but it involved a certain amount of connivance. If Gonzales were to receive a letter from his loved one, Vincenta Turena de Lara Baron in Valadolid, he might actually go to visit her. Only one person would be able to post such a letter from any believable distance - Don Anselmo himself.

Could they involve him?

Conchita believed that if the man really wanted the land he would do anything to get it, and if he was not ready to connive, then there was no point in considering the sale.

Placido therefore arranged to meet Don Anselmo in Orjena del Mar, in

27

the Bar Gloria, where no one from the village was ever likely to go.

Placido walked down to the bus stop. His car had not yet been repaired because the insurance company had not yet paid up after the accident when Manolo overshot the bend and they had crashed down into Paco's tomato field. He didn't mind. That experience had not made him any more anxious to drive. He did not miss the car.

He joined Ramon, who had the fereteria and Ricardo the baker, leaning against the Guardia Civil wall in the morning sun.

'Orjena, *hombre?*' One of them asked.

'*Claro.*'

'Business?'

'Nothing else takes me there. I am not one to go to the *discoteca.*'

They laughed. The idea of Placido gyrating in a *discoteca* with those thin foreign blondes was funny.

'What business this time?' Ramon asked, curious as ever.

'I am going to see about buying wine from Valdepenas for the autumn,' Placido lied. He didn't really want to talk, he wanted to think, because he had no idea how to ask Don Anselmo about the letter to Gonzales. He might think the idea dishonest.

When the bus arrived, driven as dangerously as ever by Pepe, Placido got in and managed to lose the others by sitting right at the back. He looked out of the window shading his eyes against the glaring sun, looked down at the valley, the olive groves on one side, the vineyards on the other and Emilio's ridiculous avocados at the bottom. What he thought he'd make out of that investment was anybody's guess.

The bus started off with a jolt, Magdalena's two little sons running after it.

Why weren't they at school being taught the facts of life by El Maestro?

What a joke that was, El Maestro becoming a father. El Cura would certainly have something to get excited about now, the old fool.

They passed the ruined cortijo Don Anselmo wanted. The man would be made to lumber himself with it, but buying property, luckily, was something Placido knew about. Three months ago he might well have been taken for a ride, but he knew the value of land now and he knew the value to the *extranjero*. Property prices were something he had gone into very carefully, all thanks to Gonzales and that idiot Leoncio.

Gonzales, in his enthusiasm to bring communism to the village and unite the people in the common cause of flattening everyone down to the same level, had worked hard - the only time he had in fact - to establish the availability of council houses for the poorer and more deserving families in the pueblo.

Under a doubtful law which nobody had questioned because it affected no one, he had put a compulsory purchase order on three old houses at the very top of the village which had not been inhabited for twenty years. No one had claimed ownership since the Civil War and it was generally supposed the owners had died.

Having purchased the houses for the *ayuntamiento*, Gonzales had then hired the services of Esteban to rebuild the inside. Water had been piped up, drainage put in, electricity talked about and the first house had been made habitable with two dormitorios, a bathroom, kitchen and *sala de estar.*

Leoncio, who had worked for Esteban, had been the quickest in putting in an application, and though everyone knew that three of his children were bastards from a passing salesman, he had got the house.

The truth was that nobody in their right minds would go and live up there, the walk alone took twenty minutes and it was common knowledge that that side of the hill was damp due to an underground source which emerged somewhere under the house.

The whole family of seven had moved in and it had to be admitted that Leoncio worked hard at making it look nice. Geraniums appeared in plastic flower pots on the little balcony above the front door, he furnished it sparsely but sensibly, and could be seen most days putting finishing touches to the roof.

Then on the cold night of February the 5th, the night when all the men of the village were in the Alhambra watching a recording of Atletico Bilbao beating the daylights out of Málaga on the television, there had been a cry in the streets of 'Fuego!'

At first the reaction had been slow. A few heads had turned, then Placido himself had gone out into the street and seen the sky lit up red above the village. Leoncio's house was alight.

Fire was a serious business for Almijara; it could spread from house to house, and once one caught alight there was no telling how quickly the flames might spread, and there was no fire appliance because no vehicle would ever be able to get up the steep cobbled streets.

Placido had come back into the bar, switched on all the lights, switched off the television and called for help. As one man the village had rushed up the hill. Not since the fire at the olive oil factory in 1828 had there been such an event in the village; then, the short supply of buckets had resulted in the place burning down completely. This time hundreds of plastic containers of every sort appeared as if from nowhere, a human chain immediately formed itself down by the village pump behind the church and water made its way up Calle Cristo past La Viuda's house, Ricardo's bakery, Guardino's bar, along Zactine and up to the burning house.

Everyone lent a hand. The crackling of the fire as it gripped the timbers put fear into everyone's hearts and for three hours they worked, pouring bucket of water on the flames while Paco's brother, the *fontanero*, clipped rubber hoses onto various outlets, and from above the house the *sequía*, which normally served to irrigate the land below, was opened up and diverted at a certain point so that a cascade fell some twenty feet straight on to the roof of the house, saving it from burning down completely.

Unfortunately, stopping the cascade when it had put out the fire proved more difficult, and it was the sheer mass of water that ruined the house. The roof caved in, the new tiles breaking under the weight, pulling the walls down with it. Within a few minutes the place was a ruin and though every one was overjoyed at having stopped the fire spreading, the Leoncio family were homeless again.

The following day Gonzales decided that the village should help and he had started a collection. He had urged Muñoz to get the school children to collect from every household and he had forced El Cura, very much against his will, to donate the whole of a Sunday collection for the Leoncio benefit.

Altogether they collected nearly seventy thousand pesetas, which was enough to buy materials to rebuild the house. Placido had cleverly organised a ceremony at the Alhambra for Gonzales to donate the sum on behalf of the pueblo, a great number of people had drunk a great deal and Leoncio, his wife and his five children had disappeared that very night with all the money and had never been seen again.

Well, nearly never.

Two months later, when Alfredo had been delivering a consignment of olive oil to the Plaza Real Hotel near Torremolinos, he had seen Leoncio with his wife and five children lying on deck chairs by the hotel pool. Leoncio smoking a cigar with a long cool drink at his elbow.

'*Que pasa*?' he had asked in disbelief.

'Life is short,' he had explained. 'Enjoy when you can, endure if you must.'

And there had been nothing anyone could do about it, except of course refuse ever to speak to Leoncio and his family again.

Pepe took the bus round the last bend of the mountain road before accelerating wildly down the straight to Orjena, and everyone leaned in the opposite direction, except old Augustin who had fallen asleep and was now thrown across his seat. Everybody laughed, relieving the pent-up fear of the perilous ride.

At the bus stop in the market place Placido got out and picked his way through the mass of excited shoppers, the chickens stacked on top of each other in their wooden cages, and the array of household goods offered for sale.

He crossed the road with the other pedestrians when the self-appointed traffic controller halted the oncoming lorries, and made his way to the Bar Gloria, which was well out of the way of the mainstream of Orjena life.

The Bar Gloria was small and rustic, with green and black check cushions on uncomfortable stools, one barman and silence. Nothing like the Alhambra and twice as costly to run.

Don Anselmo was already there waiting for him.

'I could have given you a liftdown,' he said, standing up to greet Placido.

'But I did not want to be seen with you, señor.'

'I thought it might be something like that.'

They shook hands and Don Anselmo asked him what he would like to drink.

'*Café con leche.*'

They sat down and Don Anselmo wasted no time.

'So, what is the problem?'

'The problem is that we have a mayor, Gonzales, my brother-in-law, who can be a little tonto.'

'And he will make difficulties about you selling the land?'

'No, not that. He will make difficulties for you to build on it.'

'Hah!'

'If he is there.'

'What if he is not there?'

'Then I am usually in charge.'

'I understand,' said Don Anselmo.

Both paused while the *camerero* brought Placido his coffee, and a cold beer for Don Anselmo.

Placido took his time unwrapping the sugar cube, dropping it into the shallow cup and watching it melt, stirring it. He wanted to sense whether Don Anselmo would be party to a deception or not.

'Is there a way that the mayor can be persuaded to take a holiday?'

Don Anselmo was his man.

'There is. But it needs a little thought, a little preparation, which might not necessarily have the right results.'

'Could it have the wrong results?'

'No. No risks are involved.'

'What do you want me to do then?' Don Alselmo said, straight out.

'Write a letter and have it posted from as far North as possible.'

'A letter from me, or supposedly from someone else?'

Placido took a deep breath, sipped the hot coffee and noticed his hand was trembling when he put the cup down.

'A love letter.'

'I am good at writing love letters,' Don Anselmo said. 'I used to write many for the wounded in hospital during the war.'

It was marvellous to be able to talk to an intelligent man who understood the subtleties of life so quickly.

'This letter,' Don Anselmo continued. 'It is from a woman to the Mayor, I presume?'

'Exactly that.'

'Then let me take down a few details.'

Don Anselmo stooped and picked up a small leather briefcase from beside his stool; he unzipped it and took out a small pad and a gold ballpoint pen which matched his watch and his lighter.

'The letter,' Placido said, 'Is from a Señorita Vincenta Turena de Lara Baron to Gonzales Prieto Ramirez. He lived with her during the war.'

'Her address?'

'Valadolid. I have no actual address.'

'So the letter should be posted from Valadolid?'

'If that were possible... but...'

'I have a cousin who lives in Valadolid, she will post it for me.'

Placido smiled to himself and nodded approval. Clever people had connections everwhere. And he told Don Anselmo how Gonzales, at the very beginning of the Civil War had secretly joined the Nationalist army so that he could visit his loved one in the North and how he, Placido, had covered for him so well that the legend of Gonzales the brave Republican guerrilla fighter in the hills had grown until he had returned to the village after Franco's death to be elected *Alcalde*.

'The letter should simply be a cry from the heart, Vincenta wants Gonzales to visit her. Nothing more.'

'Do you think she should be ill? Needing comfort, a hint of urgency?'

Not only was he a doctor but he was in a hurry, Placido thought.

'No, nothing quite so dramatic, but a hint, maybe, that she is well off would speed our Don Juan on his way.'

'My father has died and left me a fortune?'

'In that area...' Placido said, enjoying it all immensely.

He had connived behind the bar with his till, but never with as quick-witted an outsider as this. He had to stop himself from rubbing his hands together in glee.

Don Anselmo drank a few gulps of his beer, then looked up. 'I take it that if he goes you will guarantee planning permission?'

'The moment he leaves you can start building.'

'And no one else will object?'

'It is not anybody else's business.'

And Placido felt so elated, so fortunate at having met a man whose perception of people's behaviour could match his own, that he ordered the doctor another beer, and a coffee for himself.

Chapter 4

Placido, christened the seventh of June, which was no special day in the calendar, as the Day of Modern Confusion, for on that day everything seemed to happen to prove to him that he was better off living in the peaceful isolated village in the mountains, than mixed up with people from the city.

First he had been rudely awoken by a mechanical sound he had never heard before - a helicopter. Aeroplanes he had seen and heard often enough, but not helicopters, except on television.

On this day he not only heard and saw one, but it very nearly came in through his bedroom window. It was ten o'clock, the time he usually awoke, and he heard a strange noise which sounded like Ramon's old tractor, but up there in the air. The rattle of shutters with the wind and vibration had made him get up and throw them open and he had found himself staring at this ugly black mechanical insect hovering over the pueblo, not a hundred metres above the roofs. Two men, dressed in white, were sitting inside the glass bubble under the rotating blades.

The unexpected appearance of this monster had been frightening enough for Conchita to come up from the kitchen and seek reassurance that the world was not coming to an end.

Both stood there, arms around each other, looking at the creature, when it seemed to be suddenly dragged backwards and upwards into the sky till it had become just a dot over the mountains.

'Que pasa Placido, madre mia, que pasa?' Conchita had whimpered, and he had hugged her and shrugged his shoulders, quite unable to explain the helicopter's presence.

Later that morning, as he was helping Don Anselmo take a few vital measurements in the olive groves, watched by Paco who was resting his mules, he heard the noise again.

All three looked up to see the helicopter with a rope hanging beneath it and at the end of the rope a very strange object. When it got closer it was seen to be a grand piano. A grand piano hanging from a helicopter in the skies above Almijara.

'This would do justice to Salvador Dali,' the doctor said, and though this meant little to Paco, it meant quite a lot to Placido for, one afternoon, when the bar had been empty, he had sat and watched a television programme about the great surrealist artist and indeed, the black piano hanging up there in the air against the bright blue sky was very much like some of those strange paintings Dali had been responsible for.

'All we need now is a melting clock and the picture will be complete,' he said, proud that he could communicate on such an intellectual level. He was rewarded by a surprised and pleased look from the *extranjero* who added, 'Or a crutch.'

And both shielded their eyes as they watched the helicopter disappear, hover over El Ciero, the small mountain closest to the pueblo, then very slowly descend until both the piano and the helicopter disappeared from view.

'Who would want to play the piano on El Ciero?' Paco questioned.

A few years back he had been bemused by the programme on the American astronauts landing on the moon, since which time nothing had surprised him overmuch. But this, well this was something else.

Then, before any of them could recover, a convoy of lorries and cars came droning up the hill. Three white Mercedes taxis and three blue lorries were followed by two heavy vehicles with electrical transformers, and these were followed by two large estate cars packed with people.

The leading taxi stopped and a young man, dressed in white with long golden hair, a beard, dark glasses and a gold chain round his wrist stepped out and walked towards them.

'*Buenos dias.* Could you tell me if there is a road leading up to that hill?'

'El Ciero? Only a mule track,' Paco said.

'No road? On the map there is a road.'

'Only a mule track.'

'Can one hire mules from around here?'

Placido nodded towards Paco.

'You have mules?' The young man asked.

Paco turned and looked at his two mules. Clearly the man was blind.

'We need more than two.'

'How many do you need?' Paco asked.

'Enough to take most of our equipment up there. We can use the helicopter for some of the heavier stuff, and the transformers will have to stay down here, we have enough cable, but we'll need at least... twenty.'

'Twenty mules?' Paco started counting the men he knew who had mules.

'Could one ask what you are doing?' Placido ventured.

'Filming,' the young man said. 'We are making a film.'

35

'For television?'

'Yes, for television. An advertisement in fact.'

'For pianos?' Placido suggested intelligently.

'No. For a new drink.'

The young man did not seem too keen to talk about it. He was waiting for Paco to finish his calculations.

'When do you want them?' Paco asked.

'Now. This afternoon at the latest.'

'The mules are all in the fields.' Paco explained.

Placido felt his arm being squeezed by Don Anselmo.

'Tell him to negotiate a high price,' he whispered. 'These people have plenty of money, an absurd amount. Make sure the whole village benefits.'

'How much are you going to pay?' Placido asked the young man in white.

'Whatever you charge.'

'Five hundred pesetas,' Paco said.

'Per day?' The young man asked.

'Per hour,' Don Anselmo intervened quickly. 'Per hour,' he repeated staring straight into the man's eyes.

Paco's mouth opened in astonishment, but the young man did not notice. He just looked at Placido then at Don Anselmo, accepted what he was up against, and shrugged his shoulders.

'*Bueno*. Five hundred pesetas an hour.'

'Seven hundred after nightfall,' Don Anselmo added.

'We won't need them at night.'

'Just in case you do,' Don Anselmo said.

Paco was too stunned to say anything.

'I would like the twenty mules at the closest point to that mountain where we can dump our equipment and park the generators...'

Paco pointed, and Don Anselmo moved away beckoning Placido to him.

'These are film people who have more money than they know what to do with. Tell everyone you can to charge for anything they ask for, anything. Water, running errands, walking in front of cameras, photographs, cats, dogs, mules, everything. Regard them as an invading enemy army and milk them for everything they've got because they will use the village for as long as they are here with little regard to your feelings. And if they ask for food and wine to be taken up the hill, triple your prices, which should be tripled already anyway.'

Don Anselmo, Placido realised, was incensed at their invasion of the village's privacy and wanted to make sure that such people never came again.

'Let me explain to you what the film is about,' the young man now said, satisfied that he had got Paco going. He joined Placido and Don Anselmo under the shade of an olive tree.

Various people were getting out of the hot cars, fanning themselves with hands and bits of cardboard and wiping their brows. One girl, Placido noticed, had just about the longest legs he had ever seen.

'The film is quite simple. It is to advertise a new drink for children. It is in fact a modern version of the Pied Piper of Hamelin. You know the story?'

'Something to do with rats, no?' Placido suggested.

'It's to do with the magic powers of flute music, but in this case the magic powers of this new drink.'

'And the piano?'

'The pianist drinks nothing but this new drink, which is why he is so good on the piano. We will need at least a hundred children.'

'Will you pay them?' Don Anselmo asked.

'Of course.'

'I'll have to speak to El Maestro,' Placido said.

'You know everyone in the village?' The eager young man asked.

'Most.'

'Then can I put it in your hands. Time is of the essence and I have to get all this up the hill.'

'Trust me,' Placido said, he started to walk back to the pueblo with Don Anselmo.

Placido set himself up as a negotiator for everyone, charging an agreed five per cent as agent and an additional five per cent when no one was looking.

He negotiated for Paco, Ramon and Emilio who supplied the mules, taking the cameras and equipment up the hill. He negotiated with Manuel to supply more electric cables, with old Bautista the goat herd for decorative goats, with Ricardo for supplying bread, with himself for supplying wine, with Rosario for supplying cold chicken and with Magdalena for supplying salads. Conchita and Manolo worked furiously in the Alhambra kitchen preparing the first packed lunches Almijara had ever seen. It was bonanza time, and he negotiated with non-existant land owners for the right of way to use the path on the southern face of El Ciero.

Muñoz, once approached and briefed, was uncertain what to tell his children. Films and the cinema were something he knew little about, in fact he had only seen six films in his life, one had been Greta Garbo in 'La Reina Christina', and the other five he did not remember. 'Mickey Mouse' and 'Laurel and Hardy' had been shown at the cinema, but he knew that the children with their incessant watching of television were more knowledgeable about that world than he, so prudently he decided not to tell them anything at all.

He gave them the day off, because it was educational for them to be involved in something new, they would all have to write an essay about it *mañana*, he told them, so at all times they should be observant, and he realised that with the excitement of all these new machines in and around the village it would be impossible to keep their attention anyway.

As Don Anselmo had foreseen, by nightfall nothing was ready, so the young man, who turned out to be the director, appropriately took over the cinema as his headquarters, and it was there, at around ten the next morning, that everyone had to assemble.

He explained to a packed house of children and mothers that the story, which would only last a minute on the screen, was of this lonely pianist on the hill who, during a thunderstorm, wrote some pretty heavy music, rather like Wagner, which nobody understood, but that when refreshed after drinking the new drink, wrote sprightly tunes which turned a herd of goats into beautiful children all dressed in bright colours.

The film company had brought the costumes, bright greens, blues, yellow, all colours of the rainbow, which pleased everyone immensely, though Teresita poked Mercedes in the eye because they both wanted to wear the same pink dress.

By twelve noon the whole village had gathered on the slopes of El Ciero to stare in disbelief at the amazing network of cables and wires which supplied the power for all the lighting equipment and giant fans which were to create the storm.

The first sequence was very simple: when the director blew a whistle, old Bautista was to lead his herd of goats round the slope towards the pianist sitting at his piano on the hill.

When the whistle blew, the whole village shouted at old Bautista so that a tremendous roar of screams echoed and re-echoed round El Ciero and the neighbouring valleys, somewhat irritating the director, the sound man, the camera man and the professional actors, who were all apparently very sensitive to noise.

Old Bautista dutifully started walking, but unfortunately not one of his goats followed him. They were on strange land and had found some healthy grazing right where they were and saw no reason whatsoever why they should move.

The director threw up his hands in despair and all the children clapped old Bautista for his performance.

The director waved Placido over.

'He has to be followed by his goats. Can he not guarantee that the goats will follow him?'

Placido had a word with Bautista and returned.

'Only if he has a Billy goat.'

'Then get a Billy!'

Placido negotiated with old Bautista's brother for the use of the Billy, charging double, and at half past four, when the sun was in the wrong place, the director ran through a quick rehearsal.

Bautista's brother held the Billy and released it on a given signal. Old Bautista started round the slope when the whistle blew, his brother released the Billy who followed Bautista, and the goats, endowed with a natural herd instinct, followed the Billy.

The director was delighted. He shouted to everyone through his megaphone to go back to their original places and at eight, as the sun was just going down, the film crew went into a frenzy of activity and all was set to actually shoot the scene.

The director blew his whistle. The village shouted at old Bautista and old Bautista moved forward, then his brother released the Billy.

Suddenly, as the herd of goats dutifully followed the Billy, rubber pipes stretched above the area twitched and a massive quantity of water thundered down on old Bautista and all his goats. In a panic at this unexpected outburst of rain - the act of a wrathful God - old Bautista doubled back to seek shelter among some trees, the Billy bolted in another direction, and the goats ran into each other and into the camera knocking the equipment over and causing more havoc than the animals stampeding to Noah's Ark on the day of the Flood.

The young director went quite mad, pulling at his hair and beating his breast. 'Why did he turn round? Why did he turn around?'

'The rain?' Placido suggested.

'But he's supposed to be in the rain!'

'Nobody told him, nobody told anyone.'

'Cut!' Screamed the director belatedly, and the downpour suddenly stopped.

'The whole idea is that the goat herd and the goats should come out of the rain and be seen through the mist as ghostly wet figures. Now it's too late because the sun's gone down!'

'Ah,' said Placido sympathetically, looking up at the sky. 'Maybe tomorrow you won't need all these cables and hose pipes, because tomorrow, from the look of those clouds, I would expect natural rain.'

Then old Bautista came up to Placido and complained. The goats had suffered a psychological shock from the unexpected change of weather. They would have to be compensated.

'The goats can go and get stuffed!' the director said, and old Bautista addressed him directly.

'You don't want my goats anymore?'

'Of course I want them, first thing tomorrow.'

'Then I would be more polite to them!'

'They're lovely goats,' said the director smiling at the smelly wet animals. And it occurred to Placido that the young director with his wild eyes and sweaty beard did not look unlike the Billy.

The next day everything went smoothly, except for the smoke that simulated mist. Due to a breeze from the east, Almijara was fog-bound for two hours which displeased the women of the pueblo who wanted to dry their washing, until they were told that they would be compensated with free bottles of the new drink.

By noon old Bautista and his goats had been successfully filmed and the director and his army were able to enjoy the chicken salad and wine lunch provided by the Bar Alhambra.

Placido wandered around the slopes of El Ciero making sure that all were happy. Then in the afternoon came the turn of the children, which was much easier as all they had to do was come round the slope as the goats had done, only in bright sunlight looking radiant in their rainbow costumes.

It all worked like a dream, or so it seemed to Placido, who sat in the director's chair, just as he had seen the Hollywood moguls sit down for a television documentary, and by evening it was all over.

The next day the helicopter came out of the western sky, hovered over El Ciero for a while, then rotated off with the grand piano swinging beneath it.

When Placido, prompted by a rumour that the children didn't like the new drink and that the company would go broke, handed in his bill for services rendered, the accountant paid without checking and even thanked him for his help.

That afternoon, as the village went back to normal, except for a few children who re-enacted the part of the director pulling out his hair, and others who pretended to be the Billy, Placido sat on his bed with a piece of paper and pencil and totted up his profits.

In two days he had made more than in three months. If film people could be persuaded to shoot more of their epics in Almijara, he would be a rich man. But then he was already a rich man. It was a pity he had this insatiable urge to keep all his money. It was just the round figures he liked looking at on his calculations. Such comfort, such pleasure.

He could never imagine himself spending it.

And someone knocked on the door.

'*Ven!*' Placido shouted.

Gonzales came in.

Placido had forgotten about Gonzales. For the last three days he hadn't given him a thought and on seeing him standing there, red eyed, sweaty, uncombed, unkempt, he wondered whether he should feel guilty at not having enquired about his brother-in-law.

'What's been happening?' Gonzales asked, scratching himself all over. 'I feel as if I've been asleep for days.'

'I think perhaps you have been. Were you around when the film people came?'

'What film people?'

'Never mind. Some *Madrileños* came to film a piano on El Ciero, that's all.'

Gonzales looked extremely pained. 'Could you speak in my language, *hombre?*'

'*No importa,*' Placido said. 'It had nothing to do with politics.'

'Well next time you hear of strangers in the town let me know. Tourists from capitalist countries must be made to pay for anything extra they want over and above the normal everyday necessities. In fact, we should form a tourist board, a committee to deal with tourism.'

'Good idea,' Placido said. 'I'll be in the bar if you have any further ideas on the subject.'

And so saying he put away his calculations, stuck his pencil behind his ear and went downstairs, leaving Gonzales deep in new thought.

Chapter 5

El Cura chose Muñoz's wedding day to have his first heart attack. He was well into his seventies, so it was not unreasonable, but everyone knew, and El Maestro in particular, that it was not altogether genuine.

Muñoz had been to see El Cura to arrange the wedding and had patiently listened to the reproaches made to him on behalf of God, Jesus Christ, the Virgin Mary and the Holy Ghost. All would in time forgive him and Angustias for having committed such a cardinal sin, but only if they lived apart for one whole year and attended mass every morning for that period as penance.

Muñoz had questioned El Cura's authority to impose such a severe sentence and the priest had waved his hand by way of saying 'take it or leave it.'

So Muñoz had consulted Angustias who had laughed her head off at the silly old man's whims, and told Muñoz they could go down to Orjena to get married or to Piedra de Jelar.

Realising that he would lose face if the marriage of the local schoolmaster took place anywhere else but in the Almijara church of San Antonio, and that he would probably lose the respect of the younger generation taught by that schoolmaster, El Cura sent word round that, providing the couple confessed to their sins and did penance for a week before the betrothal, God, in His almighty wisdom would grant him permission to perform the ceremony.

The heart attack, two hours before Muñoz was to meet his bride in front of the altar, was so timed to make other arrangements impossible that day, and El Maestro, defeated, sat on the edge of his bed with his new trousers and new shirt on, but as yet no collar, wondering how he would break the news to Angustias, who was right then at the Alhambra helping Conchita prepare the fiesta to follow the nuptials.

Hurt, saddened by the turn of events, and feeling uncomfortable at having made a fighting enemy of El Cura, Muñoz fixed his wing collar and tie, slipped on his new jacket and, hatless, left the schoolhouse for the Alhambra.

Placido was there of course, his daughter Maria, Conchita, Magdalena, Rosario, Manolo, Emilio, Paco and Angustias.

'El Cura is ill,' he told her. 'Pepito the altar boy has just come to tell me. He has had a heart attack and won't be able to marry us.'

'*No importa*,' Angustias said, expertly flipping a *tortilla* from frying pan to plate.

'*No importa*? What do you mean. Of course it matters!'

'We'll get married next week. We'll have the celebration today, and get married when he's better, or if he dies then we'll get the new Cura to marry us. That old fool is not going to spoil my wedding day.'

'But...' Muñoz started.

'But nothing Miguel *cariño*,' Angustias said moving him out of the way so that she would have more room to slice the Serrano ham. 'Because El Cura does not make the sign of the cross and all that ritual over our heads today does not mean that we are not married in the eyes of God - or anyone else's eyes *hombre*! I am pregnant and as far as I am concerned I am married. Now go away and smoke one of your cigars till we are ready for you and thank Placido because he has given us six bottles of champagne free. And you know what that must mean to him.'

Muñoz, more surprised at himself for not having foreseen that this is how Angustias would react than at her reaction itself, smiled timidly at all those present, thanked Placido for his gift and left.

In the square he met La Viuda Bendicion and her husband Sargento Javier, who were discussing the tragedy with Dolores of the Caramelos.

'*Lo siento muchisimo*,' Viuda Benedicion said to him, not totally unable to hide the pleasure the trying circumstances gave her.

'*No importa*,' Muñoz said. 'We will celebrate the wedding today and get married another time.'

He had learned the art of sounding nonchalant, and it gave him much joy to practise it, especially for the benefit of such a narrow-minded hypocrite as that woman.

La Viuda gasped, and gripping her husband's military sleeve, made quickly for El Cura's house where, no doubt Muñoz thought, all hell would once more be let loose.

The news that El Cura had recovered sufficiently to get up from his sick bed and perform the ceremony after all, came via Pepito again just as Placido had opened the first bottle of wine.

'El Cura is waiting in the church now,' the young altar boy said to the somewhat stunned guests, and Muñoz debated with himself whether he would cock a snook at the priest and tell him to wait, or confirm and take his gathering with him to the church.

Angustias made the decision.

'Tell El Cura we are coming immediately, but that first I must go and put on my wedding dress.'

The altar boy ran off, everyone had a quick drink, then piled out into the street in a somewhat disorganised procession, Muñoz leading Angustias who was still wearing her apron.

Placido remaining behind, slammed a few corks into the unfinished bottles, closed and locked the doors of the bar and followed at a distance. For him the wedding had started five days before and was now definitely promising to be an occasion to remember.

He had been touched when El Maestro had first come to ask him to organise the festivity. Though they had never been declared enemies, they had never been the best of friends, but then old Miguel Muñoz was changing.

On the Tuesday when he had been cleaning up the bar after the mid-day business, Alfonso had come in with his usual bundles of boxes from the market. He sold everything in plastic, but mainly toys.

'How was business?' Placido asked as usual.

'Bad. And I am bound to make a loss this week. I bought a parcel of balloons in Jelar, and in this heat I can't display them, they stick together and melt.' He brought out a box and showed the gummy rubber to Placido.

'How many do you have?'

'Three hundred.'

'How much? Make me a price and I'll buy a hundred. We could use them to decorate the place for El Maestro's wedding.'

'El Maestro getting married?'

Not too surprisingly after several free drinks Alfonso gave Placido the box of balloons and later, when Conchita and Pilar the cleaner heard that they were going to make Muñoz's wedding more colourful, Pilar immediately said that decorating the church with coloured balloons would not be right, best to have all white balloons in the church.

'I never said anything about the church, *mujer*,' Placido had remonstrated, and Pilar had been a bit disappointed because the idea of crowding the church with white balloons was a nice one for a wedding, and no one had thought anything more about it.

Seven children had come to help blow up the coloured balloons and decorate the restaurant room. Placido had put on his best grey suit, his white shirt and brown check tie, Conchita had polished his shoes, and then dressed in a dark blue and white patterned dress, coloured her cheeks with rouge, and even put a white carnation in her hair which made her look '*muy flamenca*.'

Placido caught up with everyone just as they were entering the church, aware that Magdalena and Rosario had gone with Angustias to the schoolhouse to help her change.

Inside the church it was dark and cool and comparatively silent. El Cura, pale with his biretta and dark glasses, sat on the edge of a chair between two altar boys. He was probably the only person in the village who found it hard to get sympathy on such occasions, mainly because he had imposed so many pointless penances on everyone when they were children.

Heads turned round and there was a general titter in the congregation. Placido looked over his shoulder and was astounded to see Angustias in a long white dress and a long veil looking as angelic as a twelve year old. The dress bulged in a great number of places, the buttons on the front did not quite do up, but the laughter in her eyes, her hardly controlled giggle at the whole idea of getting married at all, was infectious and caused everyone to smile at everyone else, until they saw El Cura getting to his feet. The look on his face told them that on no account was this ceremony to be regarded as a happy occasion.

He took his time of course, occasionally sitting down during the whole tedious ritual to remind everyone just how ill he was.

As it all came to an end Placido heard a curious noise behind him, a hissing, or rather a blowing sound, and when the now married bride and bridegroom were ready to leave the church, he was astonished to see six children on either side of the aisle forming a white arch by holding out long sausage-shaped translucent balloons, and a beaming Pilar close to them.

Giggles spread through the church, embarrassed men looked at their shoes, some women looked up in astonishment and marvelled, Angustias started laughing coarsely and dug Muñoz in the ribs so hard that she winded him.

As Placido followed the couple out and passed Pilar, she whispered, 'I got them, you see I found white balloons. My Juanito in the military brought them back with him last time he was on leave. He has a whole drawer full of them next to his bed!'

And in the vestry, while taking off his robes, El Cura suffered his second heart attack which even he, this time, feared might be genuine.

That night, at the height of the fiesta, when Angustias was forcing Muñoz to dance a *Sevillana* in the middle of the Alhambra restaurant room, the wild hand clapping and foot stamping awoke Gonzales from his seventh alcoholic stupor in a row.

It was all right for Placido and the rest of the pueblo to regard him as a failure of a mayor behind his back, what they did not realise was that he knew how much of a failure he was.

Which was why he drank. How else to escape being in the way? Being grateful to his sister and his brother-in-law. If only someone or something would take him away from this hell-hole of a village.

They didn't care about politics, they didn't care about education, or about improving their minds, they were peasants, beautiful, peace-loving peasants, well-balanced human beings who didn't need his help, who didn't need him. And he swung his numbed legs to the floor and staggered down the stairs to the bar where he would drink himself into an eighth stupor until, perhaps, the good Lord released him.

Leaning against a wall, clutching a satchel of the week's undelivered letters was Eduardo the post boy from Orjena.

'I have a letter for you *señor*,' he said with a thick tongue through thick lips.

'From Madrid *niño*? From the government?' Roared Gonzales, feeling his status still mattered to some.

'No *señor*, from Valadolid. It is perfumed and smells of *Dama de Noche*.'

And Gonzales exchanged glances with Placido who chanced to be rinsing glasses behind the bar.

'Valadolid, *niño*? Give it to me!'

Gonzales ripped open the blue envelope after inhaling its heady scent, unfolded the crisp blue letter and read the mauve ink with wild amorous eyes.

He turned to Placido.

'It is from Vincenta! She wants me to visit her.'

'Then visit her *hombre*, visit her,' Placido said generously.

'She needs me, she says, an uncle has died and left her money but with it many problems. She needs a man to help her.'

'Then go and help her Gonzales, go and help her. I can look after the pueblo business for a week or two.'

Could he leave Placido to do all the work? Was it fair? Was this not the gift from heaven he had prayed for. Vincenta asking him to visit her.

47

'How would I get there?' He asked, aware that his eyes were filling with tears of emotion. He relied so much on Placido. He had already been given money but he would need more, the train fare alone would cost him what he had.

'I'll lend you what you need *hombre*. You need a break, it will do you good. Think no more about it, but just go.'

And surprisingly, he saw Placido open a new bottle of cognac and place it on the bar in front of him with an empty glass.

'Now just drink to El Maestro and Angustia's wedding. You've missed most of the celebrations and need to catch up.'

Chapter 6

Gonzales left on the day the gypsies came to town, the eve of San Juan. As he was waved off by Conchita and Placido in Pepe's bus, with a new suitcase, a clean shirt, a spare pair of trousers and enough money in his pocket to guarantee he would not have to return for at least a month, the gypsies came up the hill from the direction of Granada.

The *gitanos* were a worry to half the village, for tradition had it that they stole young children, boiled them in salt water and ate them, yet they were also regarded as the fire of Spain, they brought with them music, vigour, *cante hondo* and flamenco dancing.

They arrived on horseback, on mules and on foot to sell their vividly coloured *vestidos de gitanos* and their entertainment. Their skins were darker, their hair blacker than anyone else's, the men small and lithe, the women supple with large olive-shaped eyes that dared any man to ignore them.

They were regarded by some as evil sex symbols, by others as thieves and vagabonds, by most with distrust. The men would rape the women, some hoped, the women would take away the unwary husbands.

When they came to a village they occupied it completely for the few days they were there, settling down in the main square and camping in the narrow streets around it. Though some in the pueblo wished they would go away, many more enjoyed the gaiety they brought with them. The gypsies meant a fiesta and only the dull in heart truly objected.

That evening, in young Terrisita's house, her mother was nervous, her father was not.

He knew the gypsies, had mixed with them many times before, for they always visited Almijara at the same time each year and he had no fear of the stories about them.

The last time they had been in the pueblo he had bought Teresita a gypsy dress so that she could join in the dancing with the other children whose parents were less superstitious. And now, with the dress lengthened because she had grown, a comb in her pinned-back hair, rouge on her cheek-bones, a touch of lipstick, black pencil lines round the eyes, the diminutive flamenco señorita in her red and white polka-dot costume stepped out that night in small white high-heeled shoes to wave her arms above her head, click her plastic castanets and melt the heart of anyone who set eyes on her in the village square.

El Maestro, who the year before had enough trouble with Teresita to last him a lifetime, avoided looking at her, but twelve-year-old Juan-Ramon was much taken by her and, following his gypsy father's example of going after what you wanted without hesitation, stamped out of the crowd in front of her, circled her several times like a proud arab horse, stared into her eyes and dared her refuse him the dance.

Teresita, to the delight of everyone, haughtily sniffed the air, clapped her hands and danced the Sevillana to perfection, and the elders of the pueblo shouted 'Ole' as the two rounded on each other with all the panache of Andalucía coming out in the graceful gestures of the miniature couple.

Everyone applauded as the little dance came to an end, then Juan-Ramon grabbed Teresita by the arm and led her into the crowd.

Teresita, for her part, felt a very strange tingle when this dark-eyed gypsy boy gripped her hand firmly. It was something she had never experienced before, and though she thought about objecting for a moment, she was rather taken by his silver and black-studded waistcoat, the lace on his shirt front and his deep black eyes, and followed.

'Where are we going?' She asked.

'I want to show you something.'

Teresita was not all that innocent. She had seen many things before which little boys always seemed to want to show her. Nothing would surprise her because she had two older brothers anyway.

Juan-Ramon led the way down the steep cobbled land behind the school and round into the *callejon* where the gitanos had left their horses and mules. On a stack of cases and bags there was a box, and on top of the box a candle which Juan-Ramon lit with matches from his pocket. He then opened the box and peered into it.

'This is El Cordobes, the most potent rabbit in the whole world,' he said proudly.

'What do you mean potent?' Asked Teresita, looking down inside the box at a large black rabbit which gazed up at her with doleful red eyes.

'He can multiply himself as fast as we can count,' Juan-Ramon explained. 'I am going to put him in a box with a white doe and within a few days I will have a hundred black and white rabbits.'

'I don't believe you,' Teresita said.

'It's true.'

'How?'

The boy laughed. 'Like dogs and men and women!'

Teresita was not sure of her ground at all. This was an area which interested her but it was still forbidden territory at home; her mother always avoided the questions she asked, like how had the baby got in Angustia's tummy, which was what everyone was talking about.

'Plenty of time for you to learn all that when you're older. Daughters of gentlefolk do not have to have the knowledge of peasants,' she used to say, which Teresita didn't fully understand.

And to her surprise Juan-Ramon turned Teresita round very abruptly to face him and planted a hard kiss on her mouth.

'It starts like that,' he said, 'after which...,' and he turned around apparently feeling very awkward.

'After which, what?' Teresita asked.

Juan-Ramon shrugged his shoulders. 'Come and watch El Cordobes tomorrow. I'll be taking him to the white doe I've got specially for him.'

'But you won't be here.'

'We won't be going far, only up to the old village of Zuelegar.'

Juan-Ramon led Teresita back to the village square, holding her hand all the way, and she said goodnight as all demure señoritas should. Then she went home and up the stairs where her mother was sitting on the edge of her chair pretending not to be worried.

She went to bed and hugged her pillow thinking of Juan-Ramon, of his curly black hair, his fierce eyebrows, his olive skin, his pointed nose. She was in love. Instinctively she knew that she was in love. While other girls older than herself worshipped singers on Placido's television she had a love of her own, and they already had a secret - the secret of El Cordobes's potency.

The next day Teresita did not go to school. She put on her little white overall as she always did, had *cafe con leche* and *pan con aceite* for breakfast, took her school books and left the house as usual, but instead of joining Mercedes, Maribel and Suzanna to be taught by El Maestro, she took the road leading up to El Ciero.

She knew that on the road to Zuelegar she would be seen from her mother's window, so she went up past Ricardo's bakery, talked to him for a moment, asking for a loaf of bread, then when the coast was clear went on up Calle Cristo and turned left by Joachim de las Mata's house, then down the narrow path between the church and Viuda Bendicion's.

By hugging the outer village wall she was hidden from view for quite a way until she was out in the *campo* where she passed old Bautista and his goats who greeted her through a thick fog of *Anis Seco*. He would be out in the fields all day and wouldn't return to the village till nightfall, by which time she would be back home.

Teresita had never played truant before, but the agony of missing Juan-Ramon was worth the reprimands that would follow.

She vaguely knew the way to Zuelegar; if she hurried she knew she could catch up with the gypsy troupe, and after twenty long minutes of running and walking she caught sight of them ahead.

'*Hola!*' She shouted, waving Ricardo's bread.

A few heads turned and then she saw Juan-Ramon running back towards her.

He was delighted to see her and so were all his family. His strong father hoisted her up on his horse and for an hour or so she rode like a queen through the countryside, Juan-Ramon carrying her books, looking through them with curiosity, envying her knowledge.

They stopped and camped by a stream where the women cooked *migas* and everyone drank wine from their gourds. Eventually they moved on and, much later than she realised, they came to the caves where other gypsies lived, the caves where, she had been told, terribly evil things happened.

But the caves had brightly painted doors, greens, blues, reds and did not look at all evil. Outside potted geraniums grew in abundance and once inside it was like being in a normal house, furnished luxuriously with plastic covered sofas, the like of which Teresita had only seen in the main store in Orjena. And on a table was a small television set.

'You have electricity'?' She asked.

'It's a portable, Japanese,' Juan-Ramon explained, and he took it outside and switched it on. The picture was very clear, black and white, and holding hands they sat down on a little wall and watched an afternoon Western with cowboys camping in the desert by a fire at night.

Teresita's mother was not aware that her little daughter was late for lunch until Mercedes from next door called to see why she had not turned up at school.

Then the panic began.

'What do you mean not at school?'

'Teresita was not at school this morning. Is she ill?'

'Of course she's not ill. She went off to school as always.'

Up the stairs, through the front room to the balcony.

'Has anyone seen Teresita?'

'What?'

'When?'

'What's happened?'

'Where is she?'

Teresita had disappeared.

Teresita had got lost.

Teresita had been stolen by the gypsies.

Within a few minutes the story had reached disastrous proportions, and within ten minutes most of the village knew of the girl's fate.

From balcony to balcony, from doorway to doorway, from shop to shop, the dreadful news was passed on. It reached La Viuda Benedicion twelve minutes after Teresita's mother had first raised the alarm and she instantly rushed upstairs to the bedroom and woke Sargento Javier from his siesta, got him off the bed and helped him on with his jacket, his revolver and his hat.

'Teresita has been kidnapped by the gypsies! I knew it would happen. Every time those gypsies come there is trouble! There was trouble when my mother was a girl and there is trouble now. They are neither law-abiding nor God fearing people, they work for the devil, they will kill her, strangle her and eat her as they did poor Guadalupe.'

'Shut up woman!' Sargento Javier said, having been rudely roused from a heavy but pleasant dream. 'Until there is evidence that they took her you must not accuse them.'

'They are Republicans and should have been shot at the beginning of the war.'

'Do not bring politics into this. The war has been over for forty years, and El Generalisimo has been dead for more than two!'

'*Por favor* Javier, do not say that as though you were pleased.'

If the truth be known, Sargento Javier had made a terrible discovery since marrying the widow Benedicion: he had discovered that he was non-political. He did not like politics, hardly understood it, and only wanted to do his duty so that he could be left alone. Bendicion, of course had been the wrong woman to marry. She was ambitious for him not because she wanted more money like most women who urge their husbands to take on white-collar jobs and slave at a desk all day in hot dusty rooms, but she was ambitious because she liked the colonel's uniform. Imagine that! He a sergeant and she saw herself as the wife of a colonel. The climb was impossible. He knew that he would never, in a month of Sundays, make captain, let alone colonel. So now she was running the village, in her head. Every minor incident was turned into a major crime and if he let her have her way, all the gypsies, cripples, idiots and ex-Republicans would be rounded up, put against the church wall and shot.

He did up his jacket buttons while she annoyingly adjusted his hat so that it was straight; then she opened the front door, letting the bright sunlight stream into the cool darkness of the house. The way she opened the door and ushered him out reminded him of the men who opened the door for the bull to come out into the ring. There was a flourish about the gesture, as though she were sending him off to the wars, or like a proud mother sending her child off to school on the first day of the exams, challenging the world to doubt her offspring's miraculous abilities.

Little Teresita had probably been despatched off to school in a similar way, indeed it was exam time, so putting two and two together it was very likely that this would be a sinister case of truant.

As he made his way down Calle Cristo, the spinster sisters Immaculada and Concepcion rushed towards him, in black, waddling, tears in their eyes, hair dishevelled, clutching rosaries. If they were in a state about someone else's daughter, what would Teresita's mother be like?

Teresita's mother was in fact lying down on her bed unable to move, smelling salts being waved frantically under her nose by Dolores of the Caramelos.

Two of the more agile octogenerians, too old to work in the fields, had been despatched to find the father, who was working several miles away on an electrical installation which would bring more power to the publeo.

The village was in a state of panic. One of their children was missing.

When Sargento Javier reached the Alhambra, now with sixteen harassed mothers trailing behind him, he stopped, turned to face them and gently put up his hand to demand a little silence, a little self control.

'I have to make enquiries, I have to investigate,' he said. 'Please all go home and ask your neighbours and your children when they last saw the girl.'

He then entered the bar where, making sure that no one was looking accepted the proffered glass of beer which the smiling Placido had already poured out for him.

'The gypsies you think, or your exams, Maestro?' he asked of Miguel Mu-ñoz who was sitting hunched in a corner.

Muñoz shrugged his shoulders. The way women conjured up dramas out of nothing was a constant source of enjoyment and perplexity to the men of the village.

'She's like a boy that Teresita. Spirited. She'll turn up.' Said Emilio in an-other corner. He had hurt his hand digging in his vineyard and had taken the day off.

'I have to be seen doing my duty.' Sargento Javier said. 'Anyone care to walk to Zuelegar?'

'I'll come,' said Muñoz, 'if you don't go too fast.'

'I'll join you too,' said Emilio. 'Time I had a look at what Joachim is doing with my old fields anyway.'

'I'll come too,' Placido said surprisingly. 'I need the exercise. Besides, the gypsies might well turn on you and kill you. What do they do these days, pull out your eyes and cut off your *pito*?'

Sargento Javier and Emilio watched while Placido filled a hunting flask full of cognac.

'You have a gun?' The sergeant asked him.

'A rusty one.'

'Take it. Let us show that we are resolute.'

And so Sargento Javier with holstered pistol, Placido with his old gun which didn't work, Emilio with a pitchfork found in the Alhambra cellars, and Muñoz holding the flask, set off down the main street followed by most of the village women, to rescue innocent Teresita who by now might well have fallen victim to the gypsies most lurid tortures.

The crocodile of anxious, black shrouded women diminished after the first kilometres and, as the small procession passed the tiny sanctuary of San-ta Ursula, all the women crossed themselves and instantly knelt down to pray for the soul of the poor departed Teresita.

Those with imagination could hear the cries of the helpless mother mourning her daughter, and they asked each other whether the new coffin-maker, the young and comparatively unfeeling apprentice who had replaced the late Ignacio, had started to cut the wood for the small coffin which would carry Teresita's dismembered body, and how much an elaborate statue would cost, all before her father Manuel the brave electrician who risked daily being killed by all those shocks, even knew about it.

As it happened Manolo was lying full length in the shade of palm tree, drunk out of his mind with wine, when he was eventually found by the two octogenerian messengers.

When they were well out of sight of the pueblo and far from the women, Sargento Javier, Muñoz, Emilio and Placido headed up the steep slope to old Bautista's cortijo, which was always the first stopping place on any expedition north of the village. It had a terrace overhung with grape vines and there was always a gentle breeze coming around the mountain. The terrace had been so arranged that the surrounding wall provided a natural seat, and there was an old wooden table on which one could play cards.

Placido brought out four small glasses, and Muñoz handed him the hunting flask. Emilio brought out the cards and Sargento Javier shuffled them and dealt. They would play till nightfall, then return to the pueblo, by which time they were certain Teresita would have turned up.

When the sun was beginning to go down behind the western range of mountains, a sound disturbed them from the roadway below. On his magnificent horse sat Hidalgo the gypsy, and behind him, clutching his waistcoat, was one of his little daughters.

'*Hola hombres, que tal?* Have you seen Juan-Ramon, my boy, passing this way?' The gypsy got off his horse and slowly climbed the steep slope. He was not as agile as he had been. 'He was with a girl from your village.'

'A little girl?' Sargento Javier asked.

'Yes, Teresita.'

'We're out looking for her. Join us in the hunt, maybe they are together in the woods!'

Hidalgo smiled, flashing his white teeth. 'Why not? They are at the age of discovery!'

They all guffawed and laughed and Hidalgo helped himself to a good swig of cognac from the flask, carefully wiping the mouth of the bottle with his dusty hand before handing it back.

'Juan-Ramon can look after himself if he has got lost.'

Then Muñoz grunted. Looking down the road he saw trouble coming. La Viuda Bendicion leading a crocodile of Muñoz's schoolchildren.

'We have one minute to hide,' Javier said, panic-stricken.

And Placido picked up the flask and Muñoz the glasses, Emilio his cards and, as one, they all scuttled round the back of the cortijo to debate what they

56

should do.

'Pretend we have found a clue,' suggested Placido.

'She may not come up here.'

'She'll come up here just to see what we're doing.'

'What clue?' Asked Muñoz unimaginatively.

'Him!' Sargento Javier said, and taking out his revolver, he pointed it at Hidalgo who, wide-eyed, backed towards a tree and pinned himself against it with his hands up.

It was in this heroic tableau that Sargento Javier was found by his wife.

'Ha!' she said brandishing her fist in the air, 'you have him!'

'He won't talk,' Placido said, highly amused by the situation.

'I'll make him talk,' Bendicion said. 'Give me that!' And snatching the stick that Muñoz had inadvertently picked up, the widow started towards Hidalgo.

'Get out of my way *mujer!*' Sargento Javier shouted with fury, 'if I fire now I will shoot you. And leave men's business to the men. Go home with those children. It will not take us long to find out where he has hidden her.'

Bendicion, silenced by her man, retired, shielding the children's eyes from the dreadful molestations that would follow.

'Where did you hide her?' Sargento Javier shouted for the benefit of the drama.

'Maybe in Carmona's cave...' Placido whispered and, as though enlightened, Hidalgo's eyes lit up.

'*That's* where he is... He's been doing things there. Juan-Ramon is always there.'

'But it's a day's walk!' Emilio said.

'So we'll go tomorrow,' the Sergento said. 'Meanwhile Hidalgo, allow yourself to be a guest of the government tonight, you and your little daughter. Only this way will we get peace in the village.'

Despite the reassurances of Bendicion, Dolores of the Caramelos and Angustias, that Teresita would be well looked after by the gypsy's son, Teresita's mother had a sleepless night. For one thing she could not understand why Manolo had spent quite such a long time with Hidalgo at the Guardia Civil, nor why his breath smelt so much of cognac. Surely Sargento Javier, a fine and honourable man, did not have drink on those premises.

The next day, rather earlier than Placido usually cared to rise, he joined Sargento Javier, Hidalgo, Emilio and Muñoz at the Guardia Civil.

Each had a packed lunch and a flask of something strong to keep them happy, and they set out with their best feet forward heading eastwards for Carmona's cave.

It was a long, slow climb but a pleasant one, mainly in the shadows of El Ciero. It was an expedition Placido enjoyed, for it reminded him of the time when he had gone to see Gonzales and the bandits, and how he had first met Conchita.

After an hour they stopped to rest and take some refreshment, stopping again every half-hour after that, Emilio proving to be the fittest of the five, Hidalgo a close second and Muñoz a poor last. His smoking, he realised, had not done his lungs much good over the years, and he somewhat regretted having embarked on this adventure at all. It had been Angustias's idea of course, as a member of the search party he would be representing the interest of the school.

By three in the afternoon they were within sight of Carmona's cave and some hundred metres from it they were startled to see a white rabbit, a small white rabbit nibbling some grass.

A few feet further on was another, and another, and another; Placido, Muñoz, Sargento Javier, Emilio and Hidalgo started counting them all and agreed, finally, that there were no less than forty-two little white rabbits in the area.

'Ah, que hijo!' Hidalgo sighed, then he shouted in a loud raucous voice, 'Juanito!' Which resulted in everyone of the forty-two rabbits scurrying away into the undergrowth and two little human heads appearing over the edge of the cave's entrance.

'Hombre!' Hidalgo went on, 'all your rabbits will be eaten alive by snakes and eagles and rats and any other hungry creature that roams these parts. And if you don't come down I'll eat you!'

Shyly Juan-Ramon, holding Teresita's hand, slowly came down the steep path from Carmona's cave, and the couple gave themselves up.

'How long have you been up there?'

'Don't know. We were waiting for the mother to give birth,' Juan-Ramon said. 'I mated her with El Cordobes.'

'When?' Asked his gypsy father patiently.

'Last night.'

'It takes two weeks *hijo!*' Hidalgo explained. 'Let nature be and come back to the pueblo with us.'

But Teresita, dutifully loyal to her man, shook her head.

'I have to be present at the birth.'

With a deep sigh Hidalgo climbed the steep hill with Sargento Javier, Emilio and Placido, Muñoz preferring to remain seated where he was to keep an eye on the defectors.

In the cave, which did not smell too pleasant, they found an old orange box, two empty bottles of coca cola and half a loaf of bread wrapped in white gauze. In the shadows, crouching in a nest of dead leaves was a white rabbit, opposite her, watching her, was a large black one.

Hidalgo unceremoniously picked them both up, bundled them into the orange box and started down the slope.

'Come on, if we don't take them with us the children will never come.'

'What about the little ones?' Placido asked looking down at Muñoz who was again counting the little white pieces of fluff that had come out of the undergrowth.

'We'll have to take some of them, I suppose.'

'Catch them?' Sargento Javier asked with disbelief.

'A few,' Hidalgo suggested.

And so it was that the head of the Guardia Civil, Almijara district, the school teacher, the *dueño* of the Bar Alhambra, the best cafe in Andalucía, a vineyard owner and a hard hearted gypsy, got down on their hands and knees in the undergrowth, to catch forty-two little white rabbits who had only been alive three days.

The homecoming was celebrated by the whole village. Like 16th-century lookouts posted on hilltops lighting bonfires, or Red Indians sending up smoke signals as they did in the television Westerns, the joyous message reached the village and the first one to hear it was Dolores of the Caramelos.

'They've found her!' She shouted from house to house till Angustias told Teresita's mother herself.

'*Madre mia,*' said the mother, sniffing into the small lace handkerchief she had kept in a drawer specially for such an emotional occasion, '*Madre mia.* Pray to God that she has not been molested.'

It took four-and-a-half hours for the little troupe to reach the outskirts of the village, by which time rumour had it that young Juan-Ramon had taken Teresita to Carmona's Cave to show her the facts of life.

When Angustias repeated this to the girl's mother, not without relish, it was time for the smelling salts again.

When Teresita eventually got home, enjoying the fame she had unwittingly acquired, she was all smiles and very happy.

'What did he do to you? What did the gypsy boy do to you?' Was the first question that greeted Teresita when her red-eyed mother finally picked her up.

'Tell your mother. Tell your mother everything, there is nothing to be ashamed about, nothing that the Virgin Mary in her goodness will not forgive. Why did the gypsy boy take you to the cave?'

'To show me his rabbit.'

'*Madre mia...* What do you mean his rabbit?' She asked, jumping to the wrong conclusions.

'His big black rabbit.'

Teresita's mother swooned.

The cluster of neighbours went to her assistance, while Angustias slipped away to broadcast the latest developments.

In the Alhambra, Muñoz, Emilio and Hidalgo helped Placido put the rabbits they had brought back with them in separate boxes.

Rabbits, Placido realised, would become the craze for the children of the pueblo, and at twenty-five pesestas each, he would already clear an easy five hundred. Within three weeks, he could make a fortune.

Chapter 7

The signing of the sales contract for the olive groves between Conchita Romero Prieto and Doctor Anselmo Garcia Fernandez, took place in the *notario's* office in Orjena.

The *notario's* clerk was ready with the *escritura* which only five months before Conchita had accepted gratefully from him on behalf of Don Enrique who had left it to her in his will.

Placido was with her, wearing his grey suit, white shirt and tie, and she was pleased to see Don Anselmo similarly dressed. He was apparently going back to Madrid after the deeds had been verified. She noticed his gold pen and decided that maybe Placido should have a gold pen as well, though he was really much happier with a piece of chalk or a pencil behind his right ear.

The thick document of papers all strung together with thin green ribbon was very impressive and she was told to sign in several places and felt very nervous about it.

She had only signed papers twice before in her life, on getting married and when she had received the deeds.

This is what it was to be a business woman.

She handed the signed document back to the *notario*, who then gave her a cheque for the agreed deposit payment, the bulk sum would follow through in a few days when the new *escritura* had been typed and registered.

The formalities over, everyone shook hands and Don Anselmo invited them both to have a coffee at the Centro.

It was one of the smarter hotel bars in Orjena and Conchita was pleased she had gone to the hairdresser the day before. Not that Maria Rosa was that wonderful a hairdresser, but it was all that they had up in Almijara and better than nothing. At least she had cut off the curly bits which kept getting into her eyes, and it felt good, despite Placido's remarks about her only dolling herself up because she wanted to attract the Don Anselmo.

It was, of course, partly true. She liked being in the company of this elegant man who seemed so wise. She was happy that he had bought the place, happy that he was settling down in Almijara, for it was a kind of security to know that a doctor, though retired, was at hand.

Granted, Doctor Ramirez came regularly on Tuesdays for the surgery, but if one was really ill, as Maria had been in the winter with her bronchitis, there was always that panic, and though Dolores of the Caramelos acted as the local district nurse, giving the injections, she did not know everything. In fact, she knew remarkably little except about delivering babies and running her sweet stall.

The three of them walked into the sedate coolness of the Centro Bar and sat down in the comfort of the soft leather sofas surrounded by original moorish tiles which had graced the hallway since the place had first been built as a private resident.

Placido and Don Anselmo each ordered a beer from the uniformed waiter while Conchita had a coffee.

'So now you are the owner of the olive groves, what are you going to do?' she asked.

'I am going to rebuild and extend the cortijo. I am going to take the old roof off and put a new one on, and add a whole wing to it. I am also going to have a small swimming pool and a terrace and a balcony and a garage underneath.'

'A *palacio!*' she said, delighted.

'Not quite, but it has great potential.'

'What of the rest of the land?' Placido asked.

I will do nothing with it at all. I will probably let it grow wild because I love it so. 'There is something for us city dwellers about olive groves, they are truly peaceful and, when wild, they are even more beautiful. I want to paint you see, my lifelong ambition is to paint, and I am going to sit on that balcony and paint it all.'

Conchita nodded. She thought him a bit mad, but a man who had spent all his years looking after people, saving lives, deserved to do whatever he wanted.

'You are a surgeon, not a doctor?' She asked.

'Yes.'

'So you have cut people open?'

'Yes, many times.'

'Do you find that pleasant?'

'Not pleasant, but necessary.'

'So you know what I look like inside?'

'I know what most people look like.'

'How could I get rid of this fat? I am very fat you know.'

'You are not all *that* fat. And that is not a matter for a surgeon. It is a matter of dieting.'

'A diet, I should go on a diet?'

'If you went on a real diet you could lose two kilos a month.'

'Him too?' She asked, looking at Placido.

'Him too.'

'I'm very happy as I am, thank you,' said Placido.

'It would mean altering all my clothes of course,' Conchita thought out loud.

'And it isn't necessary. I think you are very beautiful as you are,' the doctor said.

'*Señor!*'

She wished she had brought her fan. She wished she could hide her face behind her fan as she had seen her beautiful mother do so many times when that officer had come courting after her father's death. Oh, she could have done with the fan. Instead, she covered her face with both hands.

'You are making me blush.'

And Placido looked on, nodding in agreement. He was pleased by the compliments being paid to his wife. She deserved them.

'When you have done a painting of the olive groves, could we have one, to hang in the bar?' Placido said.

'With pleasure. That will indeed encourage me to paint. Maybe not the first, but one of them certainly, when I am satisfied, for I am only an amateur, you know.'

'I will regret the loss of the olive groves,' Conchita said.

'Were they in the family long?'

'No. A very short time, but I worked for Don Enrique Velasco-Torres.'

'The old man who died last year?'

'You knew him?'

'I heard talk of him. His sons own the rest of the land in that valley I believe.'

'Yes. Not that they have been here to look at it.' Conchita said. 'We haven't seen or heard from them.'

'They are in South America, it is a long way,' Placido explained.

'Do you think the village will object to me building there?'

Since they had talked about the letter to Gonzales, no one had mentioned the building of the villa. Placido, true to his word, had filtered the planning permission through without fuss.

'*Qué va, hombre!* Everyone will be delighted. New blood, new interest. It is a dying village. The young are all being drawn away to the big towns for money. They make quite a bit building for the tourists in Orjena now.'

'Well, some of the local people will make quite a bit out of this tourist.'

'You are no tourist. A foreigner yes, but not a tourist.'

'I intend to employ only local people. Who would you recommend as a builder?'

'Fernando. He was responsible for building the extension to the Guardia Civil some years ago. And Leoncio's house on the hill which unfortunately burnt down. He is reliable.'

'What of the olive factory? Will they buy my olives?' Don Anselmo asked.

'If there is a good harvest. They will come and pick them as well.'

Conchita had picked enough olives in that grove when Don Enrique was an active land owner. Up at five in the morning to do the Velasco-Torres laundry, then an hour or so later out into the fields to pick the olives in January or the grapes in September or the almonds in April on the far hill.

At least she had nothing to do with the potatoes or tomatoes, those were left to the real labourers. But olives and grapes she had certainly picked. She knew every one of those trees in the olive groves, had sat under most of them for the ten minutes rest they were allowed. All during the war they had been isolated and made their own oil when the factory was closed. Then Don Enrique had come back and opened the factory, and the new machinery had come from the north, huge presses with huge wheels that churned around.

She had worked at the sugar factory as well. She had preferred it, the smell of molasses was less sickening than that of olive oil.

'Will you cut many of the trees down?' She asked.

'I don't see how you can build a villa without cutting trees down.' Placido knew the terrain.

'That is something the workmen will have to understand.' Don Anselmo said quietly. 'Trees to me are sacred and I have designed the house in such a way that only two will have to go. There will even be one growing in the middle of the room I intend using as a studio.

'In the house. *Qué va?*'

'It may sound a little mad to you, but trees are important to me. You know, over the whole world, trees are being cut down and not replaced. Plants are being left to die. We need vegetation. And I have an idea for this studio, which will have this particular tree in the middle and it will grow up and out of the glass roof.'

'But the rain will come in.'

'Only down its branches. It is a tall tree, an algorrobo.'

'The tall algorrobo? The witches tree!' Conchita said delighted.

'Is that what it is called? It has three thick trunks branching out, and bends to the east.'

'The witch's tree,' Placido confirmed.

'Why is it called the witch's tree?'

'The witch in the village used its bark to make a cure against the palsy.'

'The palsy? And what was that?'

'Before I was born, my mother knew her. She was my grandmother's age,' Conchita explained.

'Was she a good witch or a bad witch?'

'A bit of both. She could cast evil spells or produce good remedies, but she caused her own death, silly cow.'

'How?' Don Anselmo was fascinated.

'She tried to frighten old Antonio's father and no one could frighten him. Not even her. One day he found the tree in question with all its bark ripped off, and he was furious; he knew immediately it was her and promised he would get his revenge. They had a terrible argument in the square, my mother told me, and the witch swore she would frighten him to death. He challenged her to do so, and she dared him go to sleep for one night alone under that tree. She said that by morning his hair would have turned white. He told her not to be such a silly goose and made her promise that if his hair had not turned white by morning she would never use the tree again, or any tree on any land that he farmed for the Velasco-Torres family. The challenge was taken up, and it became a battle of wits between them, but everyone believed he would die for she had such evil powers. The priest had a midnight mass arranged for his soul. Antonio's father agreed to be chained to the tree like a convict, the pueblo blacksmith put this chain round his ankle and round the tree so there was no way he could escape; he was to remain there till the cock crowed the following morning. He took with him plenty of bread, goat's cheese and a bottle of wine, though the witch insisted that he could only have the one bottle and plenty of water, because if he were drunk that would be cheating. And he agreed to all this and even took a straw pillow for his head, so calm was he.'

'Then at midnight,' Conchita continued, 'my grandmother and quite a number of other villagers followed the witch when she left her house. It was a moonlit night, a half moon with black clouds in the sky, and when she got near the olive groves she draped herself with a white sheet with skeleton markings on it and truly looked like a hideous phantom. She seemed to glide across the campo towards the olive trees from behind the old man, and then she stood, for a very long time, just stood there, quite still, behind him, then apparently made a noise for he swung round and looked up at the fearful apparition.'

'And what happened?' Don Anselmo asked, riveted.

'Antonio's father, this solid old man who believed in nothing and feared nothing, stood up, reached out and whipped off the white sheet. Under it was a real skeleton which the witch had somehow placed there. The old man then played with it, tickling its rib cage, even kissing its skull teeth, till she suddenly appeared in black behind it. On seeing her, he'd gasped. He seemed really terrified, so frightened that she cackled... 'Mañana... el pelo blanco...,' and in a quivering voice he said, '*You* don't frighten me you silly old puta. It's the thing *behind* you!'

'And she had a stroke and died on the spot.'

'Was there anything behind her?' Don Anselmo asked.

'No. The old man had just worked on her imagination.'

'She had obviously become very tense at playing the part of the ghost. She was probably a little afraid of dabbling with death anyway. Who knows?'

'And the old man, what happened to him?'

'He lived on for years, with dark brown hair.'

'The witch's algarrobo tree.' Don Anselmo said to himself. ' I shall call the house La Villa Algarrobo.'

Fernando, the builder, was watching a football match from the comfort of his dark green plastic sofa in his newly furnished sitting room. His wife was cooking garbanzos in the newly equipped kitchen, his two children were playing with their new plastic toys on the patterned carpet, he was smoking a cigar and drinking beer. It was a perfect Sunday. Rain outside, slightly cold and therefore obligatory to stay in.

He liked that, he really liked his new home. He had covered the floor with the latest imitation marble black and white tiles, the walls were papered with the latest imitation red brick and the new glass cabinet looked truly luxurious under the painting of orange mountains and bright blue sea.

Unfortunately, there was a cloud over his head, a cloud of his own making, a problem he did not really have to consider but which, in a perverse way, he enjoyed worrying about.

The *extranjero*, he'd heard, had brought Placido's olive groves. He had drawn architectural plans himself to build a villa, but no one knew who would actually build it. For two months Don Anselmo had been in Madrid winding up his affairs. Now he had returned it was rumoured that he intended to start building.

Who would get the job?

It was not that Fernando was nervous of anyone else in the pueblo getting the work, there was no one else, but supposing the doctor hired someone from Jelar, or worse, some of the crooks in Orjena? That would be an insult.

He would have to talk to Placido.

Placido was the only person who had Don Anselmo's ear.

The big car with the Madrid plates was back and Don Anselmo was again staying at the Alhambra.

He would have to go up there, despite the rain he would have to go.

He told his wife he was going out and, as usual, she just shrugged her shoulders. She didn't care where he went, the stew could always be reheated and she would go next door and chat with the neighbour.

What a woman. Nothing in her head. Nothing but washing powder and children's clothes. She did not appreciate what he had done with the house, she accepted it, had moved in with not so much as a 'thank you'. She could have remained in a pig-sty and it would be all the same to her.

A peasant. Why had he married her? Because of her eyes and her beautiful figure. But then they all had beautiful figures when they were sixteen. Imagine sticking to the same girl for six years. Sixteen! He could have anyone now. Anyone! Instead, he had married this brainless one.

Her mother appreciated the house more, which was why she was always there. Not that he minded, he quite fancied the mother in a way, and she quite fancied him. It had nearly happened.

Mother and daughter were more like sisters. It might happen. But how did you make love with your mother-in-law without your father-in-law knowing? It could happen.

Such thoughts on a wet Sunday afternoon! Why was he more fascinated by the mother-in-law? The breasts? Older breasts, but firmer. She had style, the mother, and she had nice hands, strong hands, carefully looked after, not rough like her daughter's. He would like to feel those fingers going through his hair, massaging his back, his neck, when he came home tired after a heavy day's work. He dug his hands in his pocket, and tried to shake the thoughts from his mind. It was lunacy to desire an older woman who looked like your own wife.

It was the mother's smile, her sense of humour. She laughed so much, thought everything so funny. Like Angustias who had married El Maestro. He understood El Maestro. The old idiot wasn't such a fool. She might have no teeth but she would be fun. That was what was missing from his life. Fun! He worked his *culo* off to please everyone, but nobody appreciated him like his mother-in-law. As for her husband, his father-in-law, what a disaster. As much brain in his head as a pea.

He reached the Alhambra, which was packed, squeezed his way to the bar and ordered a *vino tinto*.

'Don Anselmo is back I see,' he said to Placido. He didn't want to seem too inquisitive, too keen.

Placido nodded. It was the wrong time. He was calculating someone's bill, the chalk moving very fast on the stainless steel bar, a quick wipe off before anyone could check. Who did he think he was fooling?

'He wants to talk to you,' Placido said with a smile.

'Who, Don Anselmo?'

'Who else?' Placido looked at him over his steel-rimmed glasses.

'You put in a good word for me?'

'What do you think?' Placido smiled. 'I was telling him about the clever way you were going to cement the floor of my cellars so that we could get more barrels down there, once the old wine press has been removed.'

Fernando had no idea what he was talking about. He had never mentioned the cellars before. But Placido's smile and his steady stare made it register. You scratch my back, I scratch yours. Typical of Placido.

'He liked the idea, eh?' Fernando said.

'He liked the cost.'

'How much did I say it would cost. I don't remember.' He could match Placido's business acumen.

'Not very much.'

What would the work entail? Three days with four men? Even a week's work would be worth it to get the Anselmo contract. In fact, he'd be ready to do it for nothing it he got that job.

'With surplus material from a little over-ordering on a big project I might be able to do it for free.' Fernando said.

'Why don't you go up and see him then?' Placido said, cutting out the nonsense. 'Room three at the end of this passage.' And Fernando went up, taking his cap off as he climbed the stairs.

Conchita had made it all look homely with the potted plants. That was a woman, Conchita, even more desirable than his mother-in-law.

He stood outside room three for a moment, then knocked on the door.

The doctor was in his dressing gown, there were plants all over the place, diagrams, sketches, front elevations, side elevations. Fernando had never seen anything like it.

'Here are all the details you will need,' Don Anselmo said immediately without any preliminaries, handing him a thick file. 'What you have to do is work out how much it will cost, how many men you will need and how long it will take. You must also consider the transport and the availability of materials.'

Fernando looked at the file, felt its weight. It was as heavy as a brick.

He opened it.

> *Roof - genuine old Toledo tiles from Piedra de Jelar.*
> *Reinforced concrete structural beams*
> *Genuine old oak beams - Cadiz shipyards*
> *Dining room parquet floor - pinewood*
> *Bathroom - antique tiles from Granada*
> *Bathroom 2, bathroom 3*
> *Master bedroom, guest bedrooms 1, 2, 3, 4*
> *Music room...*

He was being asked to build a palace.

'As you will see, the centre of the house is the old cortijo which I will convert into the main entrance hall, off it will be these various rooms. The terrace will be built to the south so the land will have to be levelled. Down here, facing south-west, the swimming pool. Above all, I want no trees damaged, only these two are to be cut down.'

The man was either mad or a genius. To build a castillo in an olive grove without cutting down trees! Wait till they heard about this in the bar!

But when Fernando left Don Anselmo, loaded with all the information he would need and all the hard paperwork already done for him, he realised that if he said nothing about it, nothing at all, but devoted all his time and his men to building this mansion, his reputation would be made for ever.

So he made his way back through the crowded bar, held the heavy file up for Placido to see, winked at him, received an understanding wink in return, and left.

Outside it had stopped raining, the sun was shining, the clouds were dispersing and the sky was blue.

Oak beams from Cadiz, old roof tiles from Toledo, bathroom tiles from Granada. If King Juan Carlos had ideas about building another El Escorial, Fernando would be his man after this!

Chapter 8

However peaceful village life could be, on occasions there were unpleasant reminders of the past. They came very seldom, but when they came they could put the whole pueblo in turmoil and upset many a family's relationship and even more.

When El Lobo turned up in the Bar Alhambra one lazy hot afternoon and demanded a *cerveza*, a little chill ran down Placido's spine, for El Lobo, so nicknamed because he looked like a wolf, was bad news.

Late in 1938 after the Nationalists had wrested Málaga from the Republicans and Franco's army had moved eastwards along the coast, occupying key towns and villages, a platoon had entered Almijara to flush out any of their enemies.

El Lobo, then fifteen and even more sinister and wolf-like than he was now, had been hidden in an attic by his father together with his young Uncle Paquito, who had escaped from a hospital where he had been working in Piedra de Jelar, looking after the Republican wounded.

Because his father was known as a Republican sympathiser, he had been taken away and shot. His daughter, El Lobo's sister, eighteen, had then given herself not once, but several times to the Nationalist soldiers, supposedly to stop them finding El Lobo and her uncle.

El Lobo, however, had seen her so called 'suffering' through cracks in the floorboards and when the soldiers had left he had tried to kill her, to avenge his father's murder.

Paquito had intervened, tried to make him see sense, make him forgive, but realising that El Lobo was unbalanced by the events, had left the pueblo one night with his niece and had never been seen again.

El Lobo had stayed on, getting older and more wolf like, feigning insanity when Nationalist soldiers came looking for young men to swell the army. He fell in love with Asuncion, a village girl and in 1939 she became pregnant; he married her, only to learn just before the child was born that it would not be his child but a Nationalist soldier's. Not only had she deceived him but, like his sister, Asuncion had fraternised with the enemy.

El Lobo had gone mad and tried to kill her too, had been forcibly stopped by the men in the village, including Placido, who in the end had to report him to the authorities and they had taken him away and put him in prison till the end of the war.

He had returned once, swearing revenge, but disappeared again.

His Uncle Paquito it was said, had escaped to France, his sister had been killed in a bombardment, Asuncion was still alive and she would pay the penalty of death for her treachery. If not her, then the Nationalist child, a son apparently, now in his late thirties, also hiding in the village.

Six years back El Lobo had turned up pretending to be someone else looking for his cousin Asuncion and asking questions about her child.

Conchita had guessed why he had wanted to see her and fortunately had the presence of mind to find her and tell her to hide, together with her son Bartolomeo, a strange thin boy who had never been healthy enough to work in the fields, but had earned his keep mending watches and clocks. After a few days El Lobo had left, convinced that Asuncion no longer lived in Almijara.

But now he was back, perhaps with proof that she was still in the pueblo.

Remember me?' He asked of Placido, 'the one you used to call El Lobo?'

'I remember,' Placido said.

'I remember things to. I don't forget. I've come to settle an old score with Asuncion. I know she is here somewhere.'

'You're wrong there, she doesn't live here any more.' Placido lied immediately, but El Lobo did not believe him; he drank his beer in silence, placed a twenty-five peseta coin on the bar and walked out as much as to say, 'if you won't help me, as I do not expect anyone will in this hellhole, I will help myself.'

Placido quickly went to the telephone and rang Sargento Javier at the Guardia Civil.

'Problems, Javier, El Lobo is back looking for Asuncion.'

'I'll be up straight away.'

When Placido came back to the bar Don Anselmo was there on a stool for his afternoon coffee and cognac.

'Que pasa?' The doctor asked.

Placido shrugged his shoulders, it was not a story he particularly wanted to tell the extranjero. Though the olive groves had been bought and the foundations of the villa nearly complete, the Madrileño would remain a foreigner for some time yet.

'You look quite pale, Placido,' Don Anselmo said sympathetically. 'I hope you have not had bad news.'

He was a curious man who loved stories concerning the village; he wanted to be part of it, and he had such a gentle manner that Placido found it difficult not to tell him the gossip.

'Has it something to do with that thin faced gentleman who just left with murderous intent in his eyes?'

'You saw the look in his eyes?'

'It is not a look one ignores lightly. Who is he going to kill?'

'You joke, but his intentions are serious.' And Placido told him the story briefly.

'And Asuncion hides?' Don Anselmo asked.

'She has hidden ever since he last came. Neither she nor her son have come out of the house unless it has been really necessary.'

'They live in fear all the time?'

'All the time.'

'How old is she?'

'Sixty, sixty five?'

'And the boy?'

'A man in his late thirties now.'

'That is tragic,' Don Anselmo said sadly. 'One should do something about it.'

'What?'

'Arrange a confrontation.'

'But he'd kill her.'

'Not in a room full of people who were there to protect her. Don't forget that in his mind's eye she is still young. If he sees her as an old woman with a son who is a man, he will realise what he is doing.'

'You'll never get her out of there.'

'One should try.'

The doctor finished his coffee, swallowed his brandy and got up to leave. 'Today they should be delivering the bricks and tiles!' he said, and waved goodbye.

Placido smiled.

Yesterday they were delivering the bricks and tiles. Last week they were delivering the bricks and tiles. The bricks and tiles would be delivered eventually, but Don Anselmo should not be so optimistic.

Sargento Javier came into the bar and looked about him quickly.

'Has El Lobo gone?'

'Along the road towards the church.'

'What should we do?'

'Well,' Placido said. 'The doctor suggested something, something strange.'

'Yes?' Everyone regarded Don Anselmo as a wise man. 'A confrontation,' Placido went on, 'face El Lobo with old Asuncion. He thinks she's still eighteen.'

Sargento Javier accepted a *cerveza*. Although Placido was careful not to be too generous with his drinks, he knew no harm came from giving the sergeant an occasional free beer.

'Can you take care of the situation?' Javier asked. 'I don't think the law should get involved at this stage.'

'I can try.'

And so Placido again landed himself with diplomatic work on behalf of the community.

Not too sure what he was going to do, nor to whom he was going to talk, he made his way towards the church, annoyed that everything always fell on his shoulders, then admitting to himself that it was entirely his fault and that he enjoyed it all.

Imagine being like Paco or Emilio or Ricardo and never having any real responsibilities. In a way the doctor was providing him with a shoulder to lean on. His wisdom was stimulating.

El Lobo was sitting on the church steps eyeing everyone suspiciously. The women, on their way to visit neighbours or do their evening shopping at Magdalena's, took to the back streets rather than go near him. He was pulsating fear by just sitting there. Placido could imagine what the talk would be, how the panic would build up. 'El Lobo is back.' Knives, blood, death - the old terrors of the war were only buried skin deep for those who had lived through it and stupidity could flare up if something was not done. Silly cows.

He wandered slowly past El Lobo, then thought that the man might suspect he was going to Asuncion and follow him. So instead he went up the steps and into the church. El Lobo was a religious man and would respect sanctuary, but then maybe he would think Asuncion was there already, which was why he was keeping guard on the door?

Placido realised that now he was beginning to panic.

Inside, the church smelt of incense, as always. Inmaculada and Concepcion were kneeling in front of the Virgin Mary and lighting candles, each praying for the lost souls of the husbands who had never materialised. They were permanent fixtures in the church, the handmaidens of El Cura who was now so old that he had to wear two pairs of real spectacles behind his dark glasses.

The holy man himself then appeared, his long wooden rosary smacking gently against his black soutane as he shuffled down the aisle.

He looked over the two pairs of glasses at Placido, not sure that he could believe his useless eyes.

'Placido?'

'*Si, Padre.*'

'*Que pasa, hijo?*'

'El Lobo is back.'

'Is he indeed?' Despite his short sightedness the priest had a good memory. An excellent memory in fact.

'Has he come to plague poor Asuncion again?'

'He has.'

'What can be done?'

'The *extranjero*, Don Anselmo, suggested arranging a confrontation.'

'Here, in the church?'

'No. Not necessarily.'

'We'll never get Asuncion out of her house.'

'But would you come with me to talk to her?'

'Of course. Now?'

'Why not?'

So Placido and El Cura made their way out of the church by a back door and headed for Asuncion's house, but they were soon aware that El Lobo, living up to his name, was following them stealthily at a distance trailing behind him a quantity of curious women.

Placido knocked on the door and Asuncion's sister opened it a crack. Furniture had already been moved against the door in case of an attack.

'Let us in, we want to talk to Asuncion,' Placido whispered.

'She's not well, she's with the smelling salts.'

But she opened the door and they squeezed into the darkness and followed her up the creaky stairs and into a room which had once been an attic. Sitting on a bed, like a dishevelled crow, a black shawl over her long white hair, was Asuncion.

'Today he will get me *Padre*. My time has come. That is the way the Lord wants it.'

'Where is your son?' El Cura asked, sitting himself down on a chair, breathing with difficulty.

'*Niño!*' old Asuncion shouted.

And a cupboard against the wall moved, the door swung open and out stepped the pale, thin-faced Bartolemeo.

'You cannot go on living like this in fear of your life because of a madman. The Good Lord has sent me to take you down to Placido's so that you can meet your enemy face to face. I will be with you and so will Placido and many of the village. You must try to reason with him,' the priest said.

'Why not the Church?'

'Because in the church no one would behave naturally.'

Sometimes, Placido reflected, El Cura was remarkably sensible.

Old Asuncion, her gaunt son, El Cura and Placido then left the house, and in file made their way to the Alhambra, followed by most of the neighbours, behind them came El Lobo, surprised at the unexpected turn of events.

Everyone crowded into the back room of the Alhambra, Asuncion sat down in a chair, her son took a protective stance behind her, neighbours, well wishers and the curious stood around or leaned against the walls and Placido went to fetch El Lobo who had stayed out in the street, uncertain what to do, staring at everyone like a trapped animal.

'Asuncion and her son want to talk to you,' Placido said. 'Are you afraid?'

El Lobo said nothing, but followed Placido in.

Conchita was there with La Viuda Bendicione and Sargento Javier.

Asuncion's son stepped out and met El Lobo in the middle of the room. They stared at each other in the sudden total silence.

'What do you want of me or of my mother? Our lives?' he demanded.

'By taking your life I will be taking that of your putrid father!' El Lobo spat out.

'Go ahead then.'

And gaunt Bartlomeo unexpectedly and dramatically knelt down on the stone floor and ripped open his shirt bearing his breast.

'Stab me then, take your revenge on an innocent!'

Everyone looked on amazed, paralysed.

El Lobo stared at the thin man's bare chest, aghast.

Like a gnome, a gnarled goblin, like an evil creature from a medieval fairy tale, Bartolemeo appeared to have three nipples, two in the right places but a third just below the left breast.

This seemed to shatter El Lobo.

Was he superstitious? Did he believe in sorcery? Would he dare lay a hand on a man who might have supernatural powers?

The onlookers gasped, stepped back upon each other, the women cried out in anguish. What satanic beast had been among them all these years?

'Hombre,' El Lobo finally blurted out in a strange emotional voice, 'Hombre...' And to everyone's disbelief he fell to his knees in front of Bartolomeo, ripped open his shirt and exposed his own left breast.

He too had three nipples.

'Su padre,' the astonished whisper went round. 'El Lobo es su padre!'

Weeping now, ringing his hands and bowing before Bartolomeo, El Lobo sobbed out, 'You are my son! You are my son! May God forgive me... so much time wasted... so much time.'

And Bartolomeo learned forward and embraced his father, and everyone, stunned, watched the two men kneeling in the middle of the room, hugging each other, as Asuncion looked on with tears in her eyes.

And after a while, Paco, who had been very patient with the whole scene turned to Placido and in a loud voice said, 'When these two lunatics have finished, we'd like to play a game of dominoes.'

Unable to contain his tears of joy at the long overdue family reunion, El Lobo, his arms round Bartoloemo and Asuncion, was led our of the Alhambra Bar by El Cura to be greeted by a large crowd of pueblo women.

All were crying.

'It's a happy occasion *hijas mias!*' Cried El Cura, his own throat now tight with emotion. 'Now is not the time to weep. Take these good people to the church and offer your prayers to San Antonio de Padua for having once more found what was lost.'

The women huddled around the three fortunates and swept them off their feet up the street towards the church.

'And place a few pesetas in the offertory box!'

Turning to wave goodbye to Placido, El Cura noted that the *dueño* of the Alhambra was counting the heads of the people going to his church. If they put one peseta each in the offertory box he'd be doing well.

And El Cura winked at Placido, and Placido winked back.

Chapter 9

One evening Muñoz was enjoying the total peace and quiet of his school room after lessons had finished. He had taken the Nature class, biology for those who had aspirations of becoming doctors, and he was looking through one of the books Don Enrique had left him in his will. As the *Maestro* he had been privileged to inherit the miser's books, none of which were too useful, historic volumes so out of date that they ended with the death of Alfonso XII in 1885, though he had to admit he had learned a little bit more about the Alhambra - the palace in Granada, not Placido's bar - and the Moorish Kings. If the historians could be trusted. They tended to paint the Moors as savages with no sensitivity and the Christians of Ferdinand and Isabella as pure untainted gods.

However, among the many books, he had found a more recent volume on medicine which went into some detail about how babies were born. He had never been one to delve into medical books, preferring to avoid the truth about his lungs, his stomach, the pains he felt in his back. But with Angustias getting fatter every day, he had a natural curiosity for nature's little miracle, to which he was proud to have contributed an important part.

He was following with interest the course of the sperm on a little diagram, getting a little mixed up as to the significance of the fallopian tubes, when there was a knock on the door and Paco looked in.

'*Paco, hombre, que tal?*' What was this dusty toothless peasant doing in his learned surroundings?

'Maestro,' Paco said, taking off his hat, revealing a white, nearly translucent, bald head above the sunburnt craggy skin of his face.

'Maestro, do you give private lessons?'

'Private lessons? Private lessons in what?'

'*Ingles.*'

'*Ingles*? And who wants to learn *Ingles*?'

'I do.'

'You do?' El Maestro could hardly believe his ears. He had not taught Paco, who had left school at the age of eight, but he had tried to teach his son, and that had been like trying to get one of Old Bautista's goats to go in the right direction.

'Why do you want to learn English?'

'Someone down in Orjena said I would get a job in a hotel if I could speak another language.'

'What about your mules Paco, what will you do with your mules?'

'I am selling them to my brother.'

'To pay for the lessons?'

Paco smiled nervously, hunched his shoulders, moved his dusty feet. 'Would lessons be very expensive?'

'No hombre, I would teach you for nothing, but it means much work. A whole new language! It is not that easy.'

I would like to try,' Paco said. 'Maybe one night a week?'

'One night a week would hardly be sufficient. Have you ever counted how many words in Spanish you know?'

Paco hadn't. He shrugged his shoulders again and Muñoz could tell from his expression that the very sight of the blackboard and the smell of the pencils and chalk were beginning to have its usual effect, were beginning to put the fear of hard regular studying into him.

'I can teach you a few necessary phrases like those for *Buenos Dias, Buenas Noches, Gracias* and *Por Favor,* so that you can be civil to the tourists, but a whole language, that is something else.'

'What is *Buenos Dias?*' Paco asked.

'*Gaud moaning*, Muñoz said, quite liking the sound of his own voice speaking another language.

Paco nodded, thinking about it carefully.

'Try it,' Muñoz said, '*Gaud moaning.*'

Paco smiled again, embarrassed, then apologetically bowed and started backing out. 'Maybe *mañana*... I need to think about it.'

Muñoz shrugged his shoulders kindly at the departing Paco, then returned to his book, to the picture of the foetus with very old features in its mother's womb.

His child would learn English! *His* child would learn English, French and German, and would study medicine and law and chemistry and physics. It would be the most learned child the village had ever had the privilege of seeing born.

It would probably laugh a great deal as well, because it would obviously inherit some of the mother's traits.

As it was Friday and Angustias was cleaning out the church, which she had agreed to do to help out El Cura who had asked this favour of her in return for having married them when he was so ill, Muñoz went to the Bar Alhambra for a coffee and a little cognac. It was still early, the majority of the men had not returned from the campo so the bar was empty.

'Hola Placido, que tal?'

Placido slapped a brandy glass down on the counter and filled it to the brim with Soberano.

'What news?' Placido asked.

'None, except that Paco asked me to teach him English.'

'Dios mio,' Placido said turning the various taps on his coffee machine. He sometimes worked the machine as though it were a steam locomotive. 'For three days I've heard nothing but crazy ideas from Paco. He's been offered a job down at the Hotel Playa Sol.'

'I know,' said Muñoz. He was always a trifle irritated by the fact that Placido already knew everything.

'I know,' Muñoz repeated more testily.

'He starts tomorrow.'

Muñoz didn't know that.

'He's going to sell his mules to his brother.'

'I know,' said Muñoz, 'To pay for...'

'His uniform,' Placido finished for him.

'His uniform? I thought it was to pay for the English lessons.'

'Qué va? The uniform is more important than English lessons, Maestro.'

'It'll be good to hear how he gets on.'

'The third of our old-timers to leave for the bright city lights and more money,' Placido said grinning.

'And not the last. This pueblo may die on its feet if the town attracts many more people.'

'I don't suppose he'll stay down there long though,' Placido said casually. 'Do you?'

'I'm not going to bet on it,' Muñoz answered defensively.

'No? Well never mind. I've opened a 'book' if you become interested. Most give him two days.'

Muñoz shrugged his shoulders, dropped a cube of sugar into the dark brown coffee and stirred the small cup.

'What do you give him?'

'Three days,' Placido said confidently.

Then Emilio and Ramon and Ramon's son came in first tying their mules outside the Café Bar and smacking each other on their sweaty backs, slamming their coarse earthy hands on the stainless steel bar and talking all at once about Paco the great defector to the tourist parade.

Muñoz happened to be in the bar three days later at the same hour, sipping his Soberano and bitter coffee, when Placido winked at him and nodded towards the door.

El Maestro turned round to see Paco, in an ill-fitting grey suit with 'Hotel Playa' embroidered in small blue letters on the left-hand breast pocket. He was looking very sorry for himself.

'Three days,' Placido whispered, winking again, then to Paco. '*Hola hombre, que pasa en la grande ciudad?*'

'*La grande ciudad es una mierda.*'

'*Si?* What happened?'

Paco, uncharacteristically, swung himself onto a stool and leaned heavily on the bar. '*Un gin y tonica por favor,*' he asked.

'*Un gin y tonica? Madre mia,* you have learned to live down there!'

Paco was in no mood to be talked down to, he did not need Placido's condolences.

'You know what happened hombre?' he said tapping El Maestro's fat knee, 'You know what happened to me?'

Tell Paco, tell.'

'Down there, outside the Hotel Playa Sol, there is a terrace for the rich people to drink their coffee and tea and beer, and this morning, only this morning, two old ladies, English, two old English ladies came and sat down at one of the tables. They sat there, under a *platano oriental*, a tall tree with many leaves and branches'. They sat there in the shade to drink tea and eat *galletas* and I stood watching them, smiling pleasantly.'

Paco opened his mouth in a toothless grin to show how pleasantly he could smile.

'I smiled, hombre, and they smiled back, and they pointed up to the sky. I looked up, saw nothing, and shrugged my shoulders. But they went on pointing. Then I saw, in the tree just above their heads, in the branches, a bird's nest, a nest of sparrows. So I smiled some more. Then two, maybe three minutes later, a tiny bird, a baby bird, fell out of the next. It just fell out of the nest and plopped right down next to them on the terrace. A baby bird. 'Pweep, pweep,' it went as birds do, and just stayed there, motionless, obviously suffering from shock.'

Muñoz was riveted by now, and so was Placido. Emilio and Ramon did not interrupt, but listened intently.

Paco paced his story, aware that he had a captive audience, aware that the experience was important.

'These two old ladies, they got very excited by the little bird. Very excited. They looked at it, raised their hands in alarm as they watched it twitch and squeak, and I, feeling sorry for them, and for the bird, very gently picked it up. I picked up this little bird, with very few feathers, ugly as the day it was born, which was that morning, I stroked its scrawny little neck, blew on it a little and showed it to them. And these two old ladies, sipping their tea, smiled at me, admired me for my goodness, so I thought I would do them a favour.

"You gave them the bird?' Ramon suggested.

'*Que va?*' Or course I didn't. I looked up at the tree, at the branch with the nest on it, stood back, took very careful aim and threw the little bird back up into its nest!'

'*Phenomenal!*' Emilio exclaimed.

'What a genius,' said Ramon.

'And the bird fell back into its nest?' Placido asked, incredulous.

'No,' Paco said rather sadly.

'So what happened?'

'It came straight down again and landed on the *galletas* in the middle of the table.'

'Ah...' said Emilio and Ramon in unison, imagining the tragedy.

'Dead?' suggested Placido.

'More or less.'

'And what did the two old English ladies do?' Muñoz asked, really interested.

'They screamed.'

'Screamed?'

'Screamed their heads off and called me a barbarian. Me, a barbarian!'

'And what else happened after that?'

'What else could happen? I left. Nobody calls me a barbarian. I haven't gone to the trouble of getting this uniform and selling my mules to be called a barbarian by foreigners!'

'So what are you going to do now?'

'My brother will have to try.'

'Try what?'

'At being the porter. I'm taking my mules back and giving him my uniform.'

Everyone observed a few minutes silence in memory of the little bird and in memory of Paco's aborted attempt at joining the city life.

Then Emilio asked. 'Did you really think you could throw the little bird back into it's nest?'

'No, I just thought it would fly away.'

'But you're a man of the campo, *hombre*, you know little birds don't fly that quickly.'

'This was a town bird. They're supposed to be more educated down there.'

'And it was saying 'Pweep pweep' in English I suppose?' Ramon suggested.

And Placido took his time wiping the surface of the bar before allowing himself to grin broadly. Then he offered everyone a gin and tonica.

'Try it, it tastes horrible, but acts a lot more quickly than the *terreno* wine, as our friend here must have found out.'

The following day Muñoz was delivering his favourite lesson to the class. It was about the Alhambra Palace in Granada.

'To you, my children, the Alhambra may be the name of a café bar in Calle Pintada, run by that simpleton Placido, a place where your fathers congregate to drink cognac and anis seco, where you may occasionally go to purchase an ice-cream when the *frigorifico* is working, or drink a Fanta which will not necessarily improve your teeth. However, that café bar, that seedy place of entertainment is named after a palace which surpasses anything else of architectural splendour in the world.

'He's off!' Young Ricardo whispered to younger Emilio as he lit a cigarette in the back of the school room, and Teresita put out her hand extending two fingers hoping she would be allowed a puff.

'As we are entering the walled precincts of the Alhambra it seems we are passing into a world where time has stood still. Neither the passing of the centuries nor the abandonment or destruction of man have torn from this unique place its magic charm or its supreme artistic sensibilities...'

Muñoz realised that he was performing well, he even wished that Angustias could be sitting in the classroom among the children so that she could not only learn something but admire his eloquence.

Then he became aware of a restlessness among his pupils and that someone was out in the passage standing by the door. No doubt El Tonto who could be relied on to interrupt anything enjoyable.

Without pausing in the lecture, he moved away from his desk, slowly crossed the room and suddenly stepped out of the door into the passage-way.

There to his astonishment, learning against the wall, pensive, smiling, apparently listening with interest, was Don Anselmo.

'I am sorry, I thought it was a boy playing games,' Muñoz said apologetically.

'I'm the one who is sorry. I came to see you, and started listening with great interest. Please continue.'

'What did you want?'

'Later, later. Please continue.'

'Then come in and sit down,' El Maestro suggested.

So Don Anselmo came into the classroom and sat down at an empty desk in the middle of all the children and listened, bringing a stillness to the room which Muñoz had not experienced since he had given the first sex lesson ever in the pueblo.

'The Alhambra combines in its edifices a number of architectural values which are still effective today. The fortified precincts comprise three sections, the alcazaba, the Royal Palace and the Citadel...'

He went on for half an hour, only pausing to draw a rough diagram of the layout on the blackboard.

When he had finished the doctor stood up, applauded and said, 'I have never heard anything quite so fascinating. My congratulations. Please join me at the other Alhambra for a drink.'

Over a cool glass of beer Don Anselmo then proposed that Muñoz should take the whole school, all the children, to the real Alhambra. He would pay for the transport and the outing, providing, and this was very important, providing absolutely no one knew who had financed the expedition.

'But why? Why should you do this for the school?' El Maestro asked, delighted but naturally curious.

'Because it gives me pleasure and I can afford it,' was the doctor's simple answer. 'It pleases me to give the children of the pueblo an opportunity to broaden their minds.'

And so, at nine o'clock on a bright sunny morning two weeks later Pepe drove his bus into the middle of the square and Muñoz with Angustias, Dolores of the Caramelos, Magdalena and Rosario who were to help him, and all the children of the school, boarded the coach, the village having agreed that the normal bus service to Orjena would be cancelled that day.

When the engine started everyone gave a great shout of 'Ole!' and waved at the crowd of mothers who lined the streets to see the *niños* off on their great adventure.

At the Bar Alhambra, Pepe stopped to collect Placido and Conchita and help load the cases of Fanta and packed lunches which they were providing. Muñoz had persuaded Placido to take a day off, visiting the real Alhambra with someone who knew its history could not but improve his mind.

Dolores of the Caramelos, Magdalena and Rosario all sat next to each other on the back seat, Muñoz and Angustias in the front behind the driver, Placido and Conchita in the middle surrounded by the excited, wide eyed children who, for the moment were all on their best behaviour.

As they drove out of the pueblo and down the road towards the olive groves now belonging to Don Anselmo, Muñoz looked out for the doctor and was pleased to see him standing there on the corner waiting for them to go by. The children waved at him, not knowing he was their benefactor for the day, and he waved back with a radiant smile.

Down they went to Orjena then along the coast road to Almuñecar, a perilous road which was all hairpin bends on cliff drops; the children sat rock still after a particularly tricky turning which Pepe took with such zest that all the women screamed and crossed themselves.

At Motril they stopped for refreshments and the women stormed the shops believing everything would be cheaper as it was a market town; back in the bus, the climb into the Sierra followed, a hot dusty journey among pine trees then, eventually they arrived in Granada, exhausted, perspiring, some children excited, some screaming, all dying of thirst.

After drinking a bottle each of the now warm sparkling lemonade, everyone filed up the road in a ragged, unorganised crocodile, past the shops where they sold guitars for exorbitant prices to the tourists and for very reasonable prices to the true Spaniard who knew how to pluck the delicate strings.

The tour started at the Puerta de la Justica when Muñoz, at the head of the file, pointed to a sculpture up the steep path and began explaining what it was in a voice that did justice to any guide.

'This is the great Pilar de Carlos Cinco, a piece of sculpture that is pure

Italian Renaissance in style...'

Further on he stopped under a Moorish arch and incanted, 'La Puerta de la Justica, the inscription in Arabic dedicates all that is defended within these walls to Allah and to Mohammed his Prophet.'

The crocodile dutifully followed El Maestro to the Plaza de los Aljibes, the Torre de la Vela, the famous Patio de los Leones and at long last to the Patio de los Arrayanes with its long rectangular pool and its fountain playing clear fresh water into its simple bowl.

Here everyone was allowed to rest. Angustias, to El Maestro's certain displeasure, kicked off her flat rope-soled apargatas and swung her feet into the water. Even the native servants of King Usuf the First would have known better than behave in such a way. He said nothing, however, turned his back on the scene and putting a heavy hand on Placido's shoulder led him down a cloister decorated with plasterwork and heraldic arms.

'You see these *hombre*? The emblems of the Nazarite monarchs, Carlos the Fifth and the Mendoza family.'

A few of the children followed, those that were really interested, while others stayed behind with the women to drink more Fanta and chew on their *chorizo bocadillos*.

After the Hall of the Kings they got lost, found themselves in the Salon de los Embajadores, then went back to the Patio de los Leones where El Maestro could not stop himself reciting a few lines of poetry as he stood before the fountain.

> 'Like the hand of the Caliph when he appears in the
> morning casting his offering to his wild lions.
> Oh thou who regardest these lions that lie in wait,
> out of respect they dare not show their enmity!'

'Ibn Zamerk wrote that in praise of the King... '

Then they came to the Hall of Whispers, the Armoury, and Muñoz told the children that it was so arched, so built, that you could whisper a secret into the wall on one side and it would be silently carried over the domed ceiling to a person's ear on the other side. Thus spies had relayed messages to each other even in the presence of their enemies.

Half the children spread themselves along the semi-circle of the north side, the other half on the southern side and all of them whispered at once of

86

course and nobody listened so that the messages were complete chaos.

Muñoz was aware, however, that Placido was intrigued enough for him to stay behind when the children had moved on. El Maestro stayed behind too, and when Placido put his ear to the wall, Muñoz, on the other side, whispered very gently, 'You are a barbarian, Placido Romero' as you stand within these sacred walls, you have no respect for history, you only think how much you would make out of this place if it were a café bar filled with customers.'

Placido said nothing, smiled to himself, amused by Muñoz's conceit, then as they walked out and up the stairs to a first floor gallery, he looked out through the crenellated arches and said, 'I am not the only barbarian, you know.'

Muñoz joined Placido and looked down into the Patio de los Arrayanes which was apparently covered with snow.

It was all white, pure white, a foot or so deep, and in the middle of it all some of his children were playing around Angustias, Magdalena and Rosario, who were screaming with laughter.

It was not snow at all, but foam, detergent foam. Then three Alhambra guides arrived and Muñoz realised that all hell would be let loose.

'I think we had better go back to the bus,' he suggested.

'How?'

'There must be a back way out.'

'Well you know this place like your own home Muñoz, lead on.'

So Muñoz, Placido, and the children that had followed them, spent the rest of the afternoon trying to find a way out of the Alhambra unseen, by not passing near the Patio de los Arrayanes and avoiding any of the official kiosks and offices.

When they finally got out and found the bus, Angustias was sitting in the back feeding the only four children who had not been arrested.

'Did the Guardia take your name?' she asked, chuckling.

'No *mujer*, but when I find out who perpetrated this desecration, who was the culprit, he will get a bigger fright from me than from any Guardia!'

'I'm the culprit you silly old sod!' Angustias said, stuffing her mouth with a piece of bread.

'You are?'

'I was sitting by the fountain having a drink; I put down the bottle of detergent, and knocked it over by mistake with my elbow.' She thought it very funny.

'What were you doing with a bottle of detergent on a journey like this?'

'*Hombre!* I bought it in the market in Motril. Everyone knows it's cheaper in Motril.'

Chapter 10

The two individuals arrived on Sunday Morning.

They made their way very slowly up the main street to the square, heavily laden with rucksacks on their backs. Exhausted, they'd settled down on the church steps, took their shoes off and sat there staring at all those who were staring at them.

Neither could be said to be pretty, nor were they ugly. They had light hair, not blonde, but certainly not dark and both had blue eyes. The reason they caused so much interest was that no one who looked at them could make out whether they were male or female. Both could be men, on the other hand they might both be girls, or then again maybe there was one of each, but there was nothing definite to give anyone a clue.

The riddle of what they were was so intriguing that Placido received his first bet shortly after they were seen to comb their hair, at about eleven o'clock that morning.

Paco said they were women, because their long hair went right down to the middle of their backs, Emilio thought them men because they had no *pechos*, Ramon thought they were flat chested women because they had high-heeled boots, and Felipe said they were men because they wore no make-up.

It was decided that the betting would end the moment someone talked to them as the pitch of their voices would give them away, or if they did not talk, then when someone had actual proof, like seeing them undress, or saw a definite shape. It was agreed that both had very acceptable *culos*, however Alfredo, who had a great deal of experience of *extranjeros*, complicated the matter by explaining that young students from distant countries now wore their hair long if male, high boots if male and that the females were proud not to have any *pechos* at all, which increased the betting, much to Placido's delight, as he seldom lost when in charge of the book, and even side bets were taken as to who would first speak to them.

Ricardo, the baker, was the favourite because the first thing anyone ever bought was bread. Ricardo and two witnesses in fact waited patiently in the bakery most of the morning, but the *extranjeros* did not move at all from their position on the steps of the church, not even when Inmaculada and Conception came out and had to step over their various bits of luggage.

Clearly, Alfredo explained, the *extranjeros* were hippies, students with no money, little intelligence and certainly no sense of decorum. By two o'clock everyone except Placido began to lose interest in them, then a whisper reached the Alhambra that they had got up and were coming towards the bar.

Esteban, who had gone very near them and peered into their faces, reported that one of them was showing definite signs of having a beard, while the other did not, but it was still all very speculative. They both of them walked into the Alhambra, made their way silently to the back of the room and sat down at the table near the little balcony overlooking the view of the valley.

Placido, servile, went to take their order.

They asked for two portions of *gambas a la plancha*, a large *tortilla*, an *ensalada mixta* and four bottles of ice cold *cerveza*.

As though sensing that Placido doubted their ability to pay, one of them dug a purse out from the depths of his or her rucksack and put it on the table, casually opening to check that there was money in it but clearly showing that there was plenty, mainly thousand-peseta notes.

'What have they ordered?' Esteban asked.

Placido told him 'The one with the money has a purse.'

Those that had betted that one of them was a woman slapped each other on the back.

'They are rich, and yet not rich,' Paco remarked. 'They roll their own cigarettes, one, very thin, and pass it to each other. If they can afford *gambas*, why can't they afford tobacco?'

The *extranjeros* were a problem.

'So, how do they speak?'

'Only one mumbled the order,' Placido said. 'I think they come from the north.'

'That far?' One of the sages nodded.

Conchita and Manolo busied themselves in the kitchen as the bar filled up with the Sunday regulars. Manuel and Pepe were a bit taken aback to find their domino table occupied, but said nothing. Ricardo thwarted at the strangers not buying his bread, sat with Ramon at another table and sipped his wine and watched them.

'They haven't spoken a word to each other,' the report went round. 'They've just smoked the one cigarette and gazed out of the window.'

Placido got the order, put it all on a large tray and took it to them with the ice cold beers.

They looked up at him with doleful, cloudy eyes in a way of thanks, and sat there for a further two hours eating, very slowly, without speaking.

Finally, one of them got up and made his way to the toilet which he found without asking anyone, then he, or indeed she, asked whether they could have a room for the night.

There was one next to Don Anselmo, and Placido showed it to the couple. After that even he lost interest.

As the afternoon sun baked down on the roofs of the village Placido sat down heavily in the rocking chair by the shuttered window and drifted off into his well-earned siesta. Sunday was the busiest day, always, yet it was the most relaxing. People somehow made less demands on you, were less excitable, more understanding.

At seven Placido came out of a deep sleep and awoke, gradually aware that he had to start getting the bar ready for the evening. He would be up till two or three in the morning if business was as good as it usually was, and only organisation would enable him to enjoy his customer's conversation.

On his way up to the bathroom to splash water on his face, he remembered the *extranjeros*, and wondered if they had gone out. Unknown to anyone but himself and Conchita, there was a crack in the door which enabled one to have a good look into the room just half way across the bed, and as he looked, he saw that the bed was quite empty, made up, untouched.

Clearly they had just left their rucksacks and gone out, probably on the same insane trek up to El Ciero where all the visitors went.

Boldly he opened the door and was astonished to see both the *extranjeros*, sitting cross legged on the hard tiled floor, their backs to the wall, their arms ridged down the length of their bodies, their hands crossed over their crotches.

They were quite naked and one was clearly a man, the other clearly a girl. Their eyes were closed.

'Perdone, perdone, señor...señora...' He said backing out, very confused.

They did not answer, they did not bat an eyelid, indeed they did not even open an eye. And it occurred to Placido that his guests, maybe, were Indians, very pale ones, from that part of the world where Yogas existed.

By eight o'clock, as neither of the Indians had shown up, Placido suggested to Conchita that she might like to go up and knock gently on the door. For all he knew these fakirs might be in a trance and he didn't want any problems.

So he waited downstairs with Don Anselmo, discussing the technicalities of laying a drainpipe from the proposed villa to a septic tank in the olive groves below, till Conchita came down apparently not knowing whether to laugh of cry.

'They're mad! They're lunatics. They are both standing in the shower now putting mud on their hair! They have this plastic bag full of mud and they are putting it on each other's heads. Do you think we should call a doctor, perhaps they have escaped from an asylum?'

'Here is a doctor!' Placido said, and they told Don Anselmo all about the strange couple.

'They sound like fairly normal students to me. There are many around; they roam the countryside during the holidays and go to the farthest places they can find to get away from everybody else. They are peace-loving people and will do you no harm.'

'But the mud, why do they put mud on their hair?' Conchita asked very concerned.

'It's probably henna, from Morocco. It's supposed to be good for the hair.'

'They do have nice hair,' Conchita reflected and, sighing, went back to the kitchen.

'Are they poor people then?' Placido asked. It occurred to him that they might not be able to pay for the room, though he had seen them with quite a bit of money.

'Not at all. They are probably *niños de papa.*'

'Why the one cigarette then?'

'Hashish?' The doctor suggested. 'It would explain a lot of their silent behaviour.'

And the two students came down at that moment, looking quite different. The boy wore a military type shirt, a thick belt, coarse jeans over his boots, the girl, a long flowing white dress with colourful Mexican embroidery. She had a cluster of bougainvillaea in her hair which Placido knew she had picked from just outside their window, and she looked quite beautiful.

Incredible, he thought, he had seen this feminine creature in the nude, sitting cross-legged on the cold tiles and had not even reacted. Given the opportunity again, he would react!

Don Anselmo stood up, offered the girl his stool, suggested a drink. The boy nodded acceptance.

'From Madrid?' The doctor asked.

'Segovia. Well, we are studying in Segovia.'

'Law?' Don Anselmo asked.

'Yes, law.'

Placido busied himself pouring out the drinks. He envied the doctor his knowledge. How did he know that they studied law, because they came from Segovia? Was Segovia then famous for lawyers? And what brains these young people must have to become *notarios*, reading all those papers, have the patience to understand them!

He looked at the girl again, she had quite beautiful skin, very fair, yet sunburnt. If he had his time again he would become a law student.

And he watched Don Anselmo being charming. The dirty old man. When it came down to basic nature all men were the same.

'You live here?' The boy asked the doctor. 'It's very pleasant.'

'Yes it is pleasant. And I live here.'

'I hope this place is not discovered too soon. There is already some insensitive idiot building a modern villa on the outskirts,' the girl said. 'I could kill people like that, ruining the environment.'

And Placido suddenly thought it a good idea to go and help Conchita and Manolo in the kitchen.

When Conchita and Placido received Don Anselmo's cheque covering the complete amount for the olive groves they both looked at it for a very long time. It was the first large bulk sum they had ever had.

They went down to Orjena, to the Banco Andalucía, opened an account and put it in, after which they had a long talk with the manager asking his advice.

That night, lying side by side in their old feather bed, the windows wide open and the sound of cicadas coming up from the hot fields, the stars up there in the sky twinkling away as they always did, they debated whether to keep this huge sum in the bank, as the manager had suggested, or cash it and have it in notes under the stone slab of the bathroom floor where they kept all their other money.

Conchita wanted to keep the money in the bank.

Placido liked lying in bed like this, as though out in the open, yet not. Before they both went to sleep Conchita always got up to close the shutters, 'Just in case...'

'Just in case of what?' He had asked her. 'Vampires?'

'Vampires and spirits and more likely lizards.'

93

'Lizards won't hurt you.'

'I just don't like the idea of them crawling over my face, that's all.'

So Conchita thought the money would be safest in the bank.

It was a mature thought which he respected, but one he knew he would find hard to implement. He liked to count the money now and then. He liked taking up the slab and picking out the tin box, undoing the string with its special knot so that he would know if it had been tampered with, then tearing off the sellotape, which was a modern added precaution. Inside were bundles of thousand peseta notes tightly kept together with elastic bans, and a small bag of gold coins dating back from his own grandfather, a legacy.

The box was full, admittedly, and no way would they be able to get Don Anselmo's payment in it, let alone in the hole under the slab itself, but another place could be found.

'If the house burnt down, imagine, everything gone.' Conchita whispered in the dark.

That was true.

'Besides, I don't think we should even leave it in the bank.'

'No? Where then?'

'I think we should invest it.'

'It's your money,' Placido said, generously, maybe foolishly.

'I know. That's why I've thought of investing it. I'm going to buy out Rosa.'

'Rosa?'

'She does terrible things with people's hair, and the pueblo needs a good hairdresser. I'll buy her out and employ someone else.'

'Who?'

'Maria.'

'Maria who?'

'Maria. Our daughter you fool!'

'But Maria doesn't know anything about hairdressing.'

'Neither does Rosa. Besides, she can learn. She has a good head for figures, she can run the whole place. It would be her legacy, a better future for her than the olive factory. She'd be her own employer and meanwhile we would benefit.'

Rosa's hairdressing salon.

It was true that the old goat wasn't too good at her job. Supposedly she had gone to Jelar to train but her training had hardly lasted a week, and she had returned with electric hair dryers and mirrors and large quantities of

94

shampoos and other chemicals and had convinced half the women of the village that they should have blonde hair.

What a week that had been!

Inmaculada and Conception, Dolores of the Caramelos, Carmen of the Tears had all been taken in by Rosa's persuasive sales talk. The chemicals had gone on, the washes, the shampoos, more chemicals, the twists of paper, the pins, hours under the hair dryer and one by one they had come out, not blonde, not grey exactly, but green. It hadn't been a bright green, but green enough for Paco to suggest that they would all soon be ripe for picking.

Paquita had bravely gone the next day as well. Her hair, originally chestnut, was supposed to come out black with blue shades. She longed to be a brunette; it had come out orange, a good orange, suitable for one of those actresses on television when the contrast was bad.

After that Rosa had to close and leave the village for fear of being lynched and the eight coloured virgins, as they had been called, had then cut off each other's hair and it had taken three months for the colour to wash out. Rosa had come back claiming that she had more lessons and displaying a hairdresser's certificate from Málaga. Eventually she had built up a little business, just cutting and trimming, shampooing and occasionally doing a permanent wave.

'How much would Rosa want for her business?' Placido asked.

And Conchita knew exactly. She had worked it all out, as she worked everything out. After all, the expenses incurred they would still have half the olive grove money in the bank.

Placido thought about it. He didn't think about whether it was a good idea, whether it would work, he knew he could rely on Conchita to make it a success. What he had to consider was how he would feel about his wife and daughter owning and running the only hairdresser in town, what prestige it would give him and the Alhambra.

It wouldn't be bad for business, but it might diminish his own importance a little in the eyes of his fellow men.

'Of course I wouldn't open the hairdresser until you had successfully opened the *pensión*,' Conchita said.

'What *pensión*?'

'Don Enrique's house is up for sale. The notario has finally heard from the family in Argentina. They want him to get rid of it.'

'So?'

'So we buy it and turn it into a *pensión*. As it's next door it would be an extension of the Alhambra. We're going to get more visitors up in Almijara you know, with Don Anselmo and those students, it's a sign.'

'But such a house will be expensive.'

'With a mortgage we can buy it over a period of ten years, put it in Maria's name, and get a loan from the bank.'

'Borrow money?'

'Borrow. That is what new business is about!'

'Where do you learn such things, *mujer*?'

'At the hairdressers. People talk.'

'It is a new kind of university?'

'No, probably the oldest in the world.'

'Pensión Placido,' Placido thought. In bright red lights. Well, blue or green lights. Bright blue or green.

'Sleep on it,' Conchita said, getting up to close the shutters. 'We don't have to make a decision yet.'

And Placido turned over to sleep on it.

And in his mind, his name came up in red letters again.

How exciting it would be to run a *pensión* for weary travellers, for the other Don Anselmos who would come to the pueblo, for the intelligent and wealthy sons of the Don Anselmos who would come as students.

And perhaps, right upstairs, he would have just two rooms with special services for those who could afford it, like that house in Málaga by the harbour.

He would pick the girls himself, the garage man's Danish wife in Orjena, and that young woman who sold him those lewd postcards at the tobacconist. He always had to get rid of them on his way to Almijara. It was the only time he was ever foolish, ever spent money pointlessly, but he liked going in there just to speak to her.

And in the darkness he smiled contentedly, and Conchita suddenly said, 'Placido, what are you getting so excited about? Is it my new perfume?'

'It is your new perfume, mujer. It is your new perfume.'

'I sometimes think you get more excited about me than money. Sometimes.' And she got up, opened the shutters again to let the stars in, and he saw her silhouette against the night sky, and that was always pleasing.

Chapter 11

As the time of the birth came closer, Miguel Muñoz realised he would not be able to bear the tension. His whole life was going to change because of a new human being for whom he would be responsible.

He, Miguel Muñoz, the insignificant village school-teacher who had once dreamed of becoming mayor, of having a statue of himself in the square, of getting the school a swimming pool and playgrounds, he who had allowed himself to have such dreams knowing they would never come true, was now actually going to be a father, a perfectly normal happening to the majority of people, but not to him. Not to him, because in his wildest fantasies he had never once imagined himself either husband or father. He had seen himself as a poor, lonely, unwanted bachelor, and had come to terms with this way of life, with being surrounded by other people's children, but now, Angustias his wife, was heaving herself around the house with this great protrusion in front of her, carrying his child.

He was curious, of course, to know what it should be. He had tentatively suggested they should talk about alternative names, but Angustias had laughed at him.

'We'll name it when it appears. Why worry your head off about such things now? What is a name anyway?'

But a name was everything!

One of the dilemmas of living with Angustias was that she cared so little about the things that were so important to him.

A while ago he had given up on the idea of trying to educate her, accepting instead the fact that she was educating him.

She was a nature girl. Sometimes as he lay in bed reading at night with this huge woman snoring beside him, he would stare at her mountainous shape and wonder what she had looked like when young.

She had lovely eyes, her lips were full, she had little ears, but her cheeks were fat and weather beaten, and when he stroked her face with the back of his fingers, he was always surprised at how rough her skin was.

But why should he be surprised? She was a peasant, had worked in the fields nearly all her life, had laughed her way through adversity. She had no idea who her father was, her mother had died when she was a child, she had been brought up by her grandmother, by an aunt, then an aunt of an aunt, so that she hardly remembered whom she had lived with.

He schooling had been neglected, five months of attendance altogether at the most in this very school house, yet she knew more about life than he did.

He could recite poems, he could recite poems about birth, poverty, starvation, illness and death, about hardship and sorrow, loneliness and suffering, but she had experienced it all.

Sometimes when he quoted a poem she would react.

'That was good. You have been through this?' she would ask.

'No, it is a poem by Jorge Guillén.'

'Then he knows what he is poeming about.'

Now the day when he would be a father was approaching and she was preparing for the event as though it was just another of nature's inevitable jokes. She went about her business as though nothing exceptional was going to happen, the laundry, the washing down by the fountain, the market, the cleaning of the church and the school were all much more important. She had insisted on working and could not believe it when he had suggested she should stop, besides her money and his would make their life more comfortable.

As he had entered the schoolroom that particular morning and the titters did not stop as he came in, he realised he was quite pleased. They had stopped in the past. The moment he came in he heard the groans and saw the faces of the children looking down, hating every moment of school. But since his wedding the children's faces smiled up at him. He was simply a happier man, he would own one of these simple little faces soon, he would have created one.

'*Niños!*' he barked, swinging his heavy form on to the high stool behind the desk. 'Hands up how many of you know how you came into the world.'

Every one of them put up a hand excitedly, some waving frantically to get attention. That had not happened before either. Usually no one put their hands up because no one knew the answer.

'Well Luis, how did you come into the world?' The boy was twelve, mature. His answer would be interesting.

'From my mother.'

'Explain.'

'From inside my mother. The baby grows inside the mother like your baby is growing inside Angustias's stomach.'

'There is no need to be personal.'

'Well you put it in there.'

The classroom guffawed, screamed, sniggered.

'How?' He asked.

Luis blushed.

'Come on Luis. How does a man plant his seed in the woman?'

'With his *pito*,' Luis said in a hushed voice.

'Exactly. Very good.'

And as everyone started to snigger again, he brought the flat of his hand down hard on the desk and held a finger up for silence.

'We are privileged,' he boomed, 'to be living in a rural community where birth and death are our daily neighbours.'

The hush had only become familiar recently. In the past he had got total silence by an intonation which prefaced a boring lecture, but now the children enjoyed his teaching. He continued.

'Many boys and girls in the towns and cities do not know how we are born because they do not see it. But we, up here in this blessed mountain village, see it all around us. It is a natural happening. However, there is much we take for granted. We take for granted, for example, that a man has seeds, that he plants them into the woman and that the seed grows. But how does it grow? How do seeds grow in the earth? Angelita?'

'With the help of the weather, the sun and the rain.'

'Does a baby then get sun rays and water?'

A general murmur suggested that it does not.

'Anyone know how the child grows?'

He had struck an area of ignorance which he had suspected, and now he was ready, well versed in all of it for only the night before he had read all about it.

'The first step towards a new individual, which takes half of its characteristics from its father and half from its mother, is when a single spermatozoa from the man penetrates the egg of the women. Inside the fertilised egg, its fused nucleus divides into two identical cells, then four, then eight, then sixteen until it looks like a *frambuesa* of sixty-four cells.'

The children giggled, they did not understand what he was talking about, but looking like a raspberry before you were born was funny.

El Maestro turned to the blackboard and started drawing a reasonable picture of a baby upside down in its mother's womb.

As he did so everyone heard the quite unmistakable sound of a baby crying.

Everyone held their breath, Muñoz stopped drawing there was a complete hush in the classroom, and Teresita put her hand up.

'Yes, Teresita?'

'I think you have become a father, *Señor*.'

And the door burst open and Dolores of the Caramelos came in with a bundle that was bawling its head off.

'*Una niña Maestro, una niña!*'

And all the children got up and rushed around Dolores and stood on tiptoe to have a look.

'I am the father of a girl,' Muñoz announced emotionally, and looked at the prune-like face in the middle of the bundle.

Then Magdalena came in with another bundle.

'You are the father of a *niño!*' She shouted. And a cheer went up from all the children.

'Twins!' they screamed. '*Gemelos!*'

And the door bust open again and everyone stared in disbelief. There, smiling, but wiping tears from her cheeks was Angustias herself, clearly exhausted but determined to show she was even healthier and stronger than she was reputed to be.

'*Mujer!* What are you doing out of bed?'

'Hombre, I am not sick. They look good, don't they.'

And he stared at her, and she stared back, laughing at him.

''You knew then, you knew there would be two?'

'Of course I knew *hombre*, but I didn't want to frighten you.'

'What are we going to call them?'

'Miguelito and Miguelita.'

'You knew that too?'

'Of course I knew that too. What else do you think I've been thinking about as you lay there snoring away during my sleepless nights?'

And all the children formed a ring round the two screaming twins, Angustias and El Maestro, and chanted at the tops of their voices 'Miguelito, Miguelita, Miguelito, Miguelita...,' until Miguel Muñoz, El Maestro of Almijara, could not control his emotions any longer and burst into tears.

Chapter 12

Pedro, the young postman who drove up to Almijara from Orjena on his motorbike with the letters twice a week - if it was warranted - came into the Alhambra after his deliveries, sat at the bar and asked for a *Zumo de Manzana*, an apple juice.

'Apple juice?' Placido queried. 'Where would I get apple juice? Do you mean cider?'

'No apple juice. They sell it down in Orjena. It's a new drink, so of course you may not have it.'

Like many young people Pedro always managed to convey that life down in Orjena was modern and more civilised. It irritated Placido, but he managed to check his annoyance. Just.

'They have many new things in Orjena, then?'

'Every day there is something new,' Pedro said.

'Bankruptcies too?'

'Bankruptcies?'

'I understand that the man who built all those blocks of flats which are not yet finished is a little short of *dinero*.'

Pedro shrugged his shoulders.

'And that sixty-five people are out of work as a result.'

'I haven't heard,' Pedro lied. 'I'll have a beer then, please.'

'How's your father?' Placido asked.

'He's all right.'

Pedro's father happened to be one of the great developer's builders, he happened to be one of those now out of work. Placido gave him the beer and didn't labour the point.

Pedro drank the beer quickly, glanced at his watch, and put his money on the bar. 'There's a letter for your daughter,' he said, and laid an envelope down next to the money.

Placido ignored it till Pedro had left, then picked it up. The letter was not for Maria but for Eloisa who worked the telephones.

He quickly went to the door, out into the street and shouted after Pedro. 'This isn't for Maria, it's for Eloisa.'

Pedro, now truly apologetic, ran back, took the envelope, studied it, looking into his empty bag and frowned.

'I'm sorry,' he said. 'My mistake.'

And Placido thought no more about it.

It wasn't as though Maria usually got letters. In fact neither he nor Conchita got any letters. Bills, invoices, yes, but not letters. He went back to cleaning the coffee machine, the top of the bar, the ice boxes where he stored the beer, and this reminded him that he had to order more San Miguel from the depository, and while he was at it he would ask for a sample of apple juice. After all, there was nothing that was available in Orjena which could not also be purchased at the Alhambra, if perhaps a little more dearly.

He went into the little passage leading to the *servicios* where the telephone hung on the wall, and picked up the receiver.

Though he had been one of the first to get a telephone in Almijara, some two years back now, he still felt a childish thrill when using it. It was costly, so he didn't play with it, but he enjoyed ringing through orders to the depository.

For some reason, however, the line was dead.

He shook the receiver, banged it with his fist, but there was nothing. So he hung up, went back into the bar, threw his dishcloth over the counter and went up the street to talk to Eloisa.

The Almijara telephone exchange was up some steep steps above Ignacio's old carpentry shop, along a short corridor, in a small room with a window which overlooked the blank wall of the house next door. Eloisa sat in front of the console twelve hours a day, knitting, or sometimes playing *parchís* with her friend Rosa, the hairdresser. So sometimes, in fact Rosa would do Eloisa's hair while she knitted.

To Placido her life seemed endlessly boring, but she provided a useful service and knew everything that went on in the village of course, because she listened in to most conversations.

As Placido walked in, Eloisa was turning the little handle of the console furiously and pushing various plugs into appropriate holes.

'*Digame. Digame. Oiga. Oiga... Hola!*' She said swivelling round on her special swivel stool. '*Que tal?*'

'My phone is not working, Eloisa. Is anything the matter?'

Eloisa could not be said to be pretty. She was very thin, the thinnest woman in the pueblo, and maybe because of this love and marriage had passed her by. She was only twenty-eight, but at that age by village standards she should have been married and had two children, if not four.

'I don't know what it is. Two or three phones have gone dead. Manuel knows about it and is coming this afternoon to see what he can do.'

'Can you put me through to the depository from here then?'

'Of course.'

He watched her expertly dial a number with the end of her pencil, note down the call on a pad as she listened for the other end to answer, and connect the line to the public telephone in the corner on the little table.

Placido picked up the receiver and gave his order.

'I see you got your *carta*,' he said, on the way out, noticing that Pedro had delivered the letter addressed to her.

Eloisa smiled nervously and quickly put the letter under a telephone directory, as though it were something she did not want anyone to see. She then turned her back on him.

Placido grunted goodbye and left. Old maids, spinsters, were apt to behave strangely.

As it happened, Manuel came in for a *vino blanco* on his way to the olive oil factory where they were having trouble with the filling machine. It was always going wrong.

He sat down at the bar and sighed a deep sigh of desperation.

'What's the matter with you today, Manuel?' Placido asked. He was the perfect barman and accepted that part of the job was to listen to people's problems.

'I've just been up the hill to old Bautista's sister.'

'Again?'

'Again.'

'And what's wrong this time?'

'She couldn't see any more at night.'

'Why not?'

'I'll give you three guesses.'

'I give up.'

'All the bulbs in her house were black.'

'Broken?'

'No. Black with smoke.'

'From the fire?'

'From candles.' Manuel said.

'If she has electricity why the candles?'

'Somebody told her, God knows who, that before switching on the electricity you had to warm the bulbs. So every night since she's had electricity in the house, she's lit a candle and gone to each bulb, held the flame under it to warm it, and they've all become coated with smoke.'

Placido smiled. Such things tended to happen in Almijara.

'What did you do?'

'Cleaned the bulbs, what else? And tried to get it into her thick head that bulbs didn't need cleaning.'

It was an improvement on the last time when had been called to repair the *refrigerador*. He had found it packed tight with jars of frozen water. Bautista's sister had not realised that a refrigerator could be used for other things.

'I understand she's buying a television set next,' Placido joked.

And Manuel winced. 'She'll open up the back to let the people out!'

And both picked up their glasses and drank to the health of their intelligence.

'By the way,' Placido said. 'What about my telephone?'

'What about it?'

'It's not working. Didn't Eloisa tell you.'

'No.'

That was strange. Eloisa was behaving very oddly, and he told Manuel what was wrong.

The pueblo's only electrician finished his wine, went to the telephone, tested it and left the bar saying he'd go and see what the trouble was. Waiting a few minutes he returned.

'So?' Placido asked.

'The problem with your telephone is Joachim de las Matas.'

That, Placido did not understand.

'Joachim de las Matas? What's he got to do with it? He's in the army in Cadiz.'

'Did Maria get a letter from his this morning?'

'From Joachim? Why would Joachim write to Maria?'

'*Ay... por dios.* The fathers and husbands are always the last to know!'

Placido became worried. He glanced at his watch, it was past three, he could close the bar. He moved quickly to the door and shut it and offered Manuel another *vino blanco*.

'Tell me more.'

'Maria and Joachim de last Matas... *novio and novia, hombre.*'

'My Maria. My Maria and Joachim? She never told me.'

'Would she tell you? Would you be proud to have him as a future son-in-law?'

The idea was terrifying. Joachim was handsome, that was true, with a Portuguese mother he had the most handsome eyes in Andalucia, but he had as much intelligence as El Tonto. Admittedly, last year he had become hero for a day when, as Almijara's only bullfighter, he had managed to actually kill a bull with one stroke, but then the following month he had his thigh carved up by the horn of a cow in a field where he was practising a *faena*. Now, thank God, he was doing his national service.

'*Hombre!* Maria and Joachim have been holding hands walking up the hill and down in the valley for nearly a year now. But who should also be in love with Joachim, but Eloisa!'

'I still do not see the picture you are painting,' Placido said.

'Eloisa is in love with Joachim. Joachim also writes to Maria.'

'You mean Pedro delivered the wrong letter? You mean Eloisa received Maria's letter as I received Eliosa's this morning?'

'*Exactamente!*'

'So she cut off *my* telephone?'

'Because in his letter to Maria, Joachim asks her to ring him.'

'But she could have cut the call when Maria made it, even listened in to the conversation.'

'That's what I told her, but she said she hadn't thought of it. Not all of us are as devious as you Placido. It's re-connected now anyway, and this is the letter to Maria. Elioisa steamed it opened but sealed it again.'

Placido tucked the letter with a few bills next to the coffee machine and shrugged his shoulders.

'And she told you all this?'

'I am an old friend of the family. I got her the job, she tells me everything.'

'And she is in love with Joachim, but Joachim is in love with my Maria.'

'Correct.'

Placido became silent, watched Manuel drink his wine slowly. No one had ever drunk wine so slowly.

Finally, Manuel wiped his mouth with the back of his hand, said goodbye, and left.

Placido locked the door, went to the coffee machine, picked up the letter and turned on the steam tap.

'*Querida mia...,*' the letter began, and it went on about love and the sensuousness of her lips, her hands, the love he had for her young body which he wanted to possess. At least it hadn't gone too far! But it was unbelievable. Joachim, twenty, was writing such things to his daughter who was only seventeen!

Only?

Placido sat down. Perhaps he had been blind. Perhaps he *was* blind. He had not looked at Maria for months. When she returned form work in the evenings he always saw her as she was when she came back from school he did not see her in the present, but always in the past.

That night, when Maria came in, Placido looked at her for the first time as others saw her. For the first time too he looked at the men in his bar, Paco, Emilio, Ramon, Esteban, even old Bautista, and every one of them actually stopped what they were doing for a moment to watch her cross the room and go through the door heading upstairs.

Maria was a young woman. She had fine legs, swinging hips, breasts, long hair, and a quite beautiful face.

And Joachim de las Matas was writing her love letters!

Placido was like a robot for the rest of the night. He opened beer bottles, wine bottles, cognac bottles, poured out glasses of *anis seco, anis dulce,* coffee, chocolate, *agua mineral,* he served *tapas,* cleaned cups, saucers, worked the coffee machine, and all the time in his head he was roaming the streets of Alimijara trying to find a suitable young man for Maria.

Soon she would be old enough to marry and there was no one, no one in the pueblo good enough for her! He understood why she had been drawn to Joachim, however stupid and lacking in intelligence, he was the only young man who had style, who had tried to better himself. He was even a corporal now, not just a private soldier. But it didn't mean he was suitable.

Don Anselmo came in after a day of choosing special tiles from Málaga for his patio, and sat down in his usual corner at the bar to have his usual cognac and manzanilla tea.

'Are you married?' Placido asked him, very casually. 'Do you have a family?'

'I was married. My wife died three years ago. And I have four sons.'

'Four sons?' Placido repeated smiling. And are they married?'

'Two of them are. The other two are still students.'

'Medicine?'

'One medicine, one engineering.'

Placido smiled more broadly.

'Are they ever going to come down here to visit you?' Placido asked.

'Oh I expect so, one day, when their father has something to offer them, like the comfort of a finished villa and a swimming pool.'

'They'll come for their holidays then?'

'I hope so.'

'That will be nice for you, having them with you in the pueblo for a long holiday.'

And because he was feeling generous, Placido offered the doctor a free cognac, and smiled to himself again.

Placido and Conchita had agreed that when the opportunity presented itself Conchita would talk to Maria about the hairdressing shop idea, and also about Joachim de las Matas.

On a morning that Placido decided to go to the market early to buy a supply of *gambas* and choose a young kid for slaughter - something he was never fond of doing but *tapas de choto* in Conchita's sauce was very popular - he found mother and daughter talking in the kitchen while boiling milk for his morning coffee.

As Placido came in Maria rushed over and threw her arms round him, laughing.

'Papa... you are so funny!'

He had no idea what he had done to amuse her.

'Me and Joachim. I don't care for *him*! It was only that once, when we walked hand in hand down the hill to look at what Don Anselmo was doing. You are mad to think that I would be serious about him.'

'But he wrote to you.'

'He wrote to everyone. Eloisa, Alicia, Rosana, Susanna, all the girls. Only Eloisa takes him seriously.'

It was a great relief.

'As for the hairdressing salon I think it's a marvellous idea, but we'd make a lot more money if we sold cosmetics and clothes, I always thought that the one thing that was missing in the pueblo was a little shop selling make-up, T-shirts, denims and things like that for people of my age.'

She had studied the idea, like her mother, she had thought it out and like her father, had seen the financial possibilities.

'Not buy Rosa's hairdressing business then?'

'No.'

'But where would we have the shop?'

'On the ground floor of the pension. Next to the entrance, Conchita said.

They had both thought it out, together.

All he would have to do was give his approval.

The idea matured during the day and most of that night, and after his lunch-time rush the following afternoon Placido abandoned the idea of a siesta in favour of going down to Orjena to the notario, to find out how much was wanted for the Velasco-Torres house, and whether they could afford it and borrow the necessary - in short, to find out if it was realistic to contemplate the idea further.

When Placido went on business elsewhere, Manolo took over the running of the bar, or on occasions, Conchita.

That evening when Placido returned he found Conchita pouring out the drinks and working the coffee machine.

I had to keep busy, I couldn't bear the suspense. How much do they want?'

'It's very cheap. Very cheap. Without any problem we can purchase it all within five years. I've given a deposit cheque. The place is ours.'

She stared at him with disbelief. The Velasco-Torres house was theirs. She had worked there as a servant, had cleaned every inch of every floor. Now it was hers to do with what she wanted.

She left the steam tap open in her excitement and went round the bar, and in front of all the customer threw her arms round and planted a bit kiss right on his mouth.

'*Ole!*' Shouted Paco.

'*Ole!*' Shouted the others.

And Placido, feeling generous, gave everyone a free drink.

The next day Placido woke up early.

"Who shall we have to convert and re-decorate the place? He asked, stretching in front of the window, felling extremely healthy, wealthy and en-ergetic.

'Why not Santiago?' Conchita suggested, 'he's very good.'

'But he's Guardino's son.'

'So he's Guardino's son? We can afford to be generous to that family whom with incessant regularity you have done out of every peseta you could over the years.'

It was true. In his head he still waged a competition war with Guardino's bar when it was quite unnecessary. All Guardino's customers came to the Alhamba at some time or other during the week, but how many of his went to Guardino's? He should find it in his head to be more generous.

'Besides,' Concita went on, 'if Santiago were to come and work for us, it would be seen as a truce, as a sign of peace. People like to be wanted you know. Guardino himself might come and drink.'

'That would be the day!'

Guardino had his bar on the higher level of the village long before Placido had taken over the Alhambra. He, Placido, had been the intruder who had slowly stolen the clientele. Strangely, he liked Santiago, he saw eye to eye with him about his father's lack of vision. Apart from himself and Esteban he was the only man in the pueblo with ambition. It would be good to give Santiago the job, and at the thought of being generous, magnanimous, Placido had a pleasurable feeling, something he realised he seldom experienced.

'I'll go up the hill and see if he's at home then, find out what could be done and how much it would cost. Before committing myself.'

And after breakfast, and after going to market, and after getting the bar ready for the lunchtime trade, he made his way up Calle Cristo to Guardino's bar.

When he got to the top of the hill he sat down for a moment on a wall to regain his breath. He didn't want to appear unhealthy to his old rival.

He then crossed the cobbled lane, and pushed open the heavy door, for it was always closed, a strange way to welcome guests

Guardino whom he had not seen for two years, except at funerals, was still sitting there on his stool behind the bar.

There had been changes, Santiago had helped his father out, that was clear. The bar itself was of stainless steel like his own, there was a coffee machine and shelves with bottles. Santiago had not exerted his imagination on the layout, he had simply stolen all the ideas directly from the Alhambra. But he had gone out on a limb with the wallpaper.

Placido was not sure he liked it, the fact was that he did not quite see the point of it. On the stone wall, Santiago had struck a simulated stone wallpaper, more red than the real wall's stone, but stone all the same. It also had ivy leaves growing over a trellis work. The effect was quite good, and yet it was not what he would have chosen himself. The old cane ceiling had been plastered over and there was a glaring light. The tables and plastic chairs were new too.

'*Hombre! Que pasa?* Guardino said standing up, exchanging astonished looked with two of his regulars.

Placido eased himself on to a stool

'*Que quiere?*'

'A San Miguel,' Placido said.

Guardino poured him out the beer and watched him take a sip.

'To what can we attribute this honour?' Guardino was known for his sarcasm and the news that Placido had entered the forbidden territory would be round the village very quickly.

'Not to you Guardino, you old fox, not to you. I want to see your son.'

'My son! You think *I* see my son here? I never see him, he prefers the luxuries of that brothel, the Alhambra!'

Only then did it occur to Placido that he had probably hurt his rival more by having his son drink at the Alhambra than anything else.

'He doesn't come in that often now. He's always down in Orjena.'

'Orjena!' And Guardino cleared his throat as though ready to spit on the floor, then obviously remembered that he could not do this anymore now that he wanted others to keep his bar clean.

'Well, if I see him, I'll tell him you called. Is there something you want from him?'

'Work. We're buying the Velalso-Torres house and are going to convert it into a *pensión.*'

'A *pensión*? Who the hell is going to come up here?'

Guardino asked, amused. 'This is not a tourist resort. Too far from the sea, *hombre.*'

'But not far from the mountains.' Placido pointed out.

'People like mountains?'

'People love mountains.'

'Then perhaps the world is slowly becoming civilised. I always thought people used the mountains as defences.'

And Placcido saw that Guardino, after all this time, had not changed. Any minute now he would trot out his old civil war story about the Pyrenees. Whatever the conversation, Guardino always managed to bring in the story of his war years in the Pyrenees.

'I was in the Pyrenees in 1936 you know, and I was at Guernica.'

Guernica should not be forgotten, admittedly, but from Guardino's lips the recounting of that bombing became boring. However, Placido was on a peace mission, and enjoying his beer, so he decided to listen to it all again.

To his surprise the story had changed. Guardino had been promoted to a sergeant now and was on the Republican side in charge of the hospital when it was bombed, and not a wounded private with a broken leg acquired by slipping down a ravine. He had two more wounds as well, from Franco bullets. The tale was improving.

That evening Santiago came into the Alhambra white with plaster dust, wiping the sweat off his brow.

'My father said you wanted to see me.'

'We've bought the house next door,' said Placido.

'Don Enrique's'?

'Yes, and we want to convert it into a *pensión*, a small hotel. At the moment there were two large rooms with two windows each, on the first floor. These could be turned into four rooms with one window each. But we need washbasins in every room, and a large bathroom. We also want to have a shop on the ground floor.

'What sort of shop?'

'A clothes shop for Maria.'

Santiago looked pensive, accepted the free beer gratefully.

'I don't remember the layout of the house, is it possible to see it?'

Indeed, it was possible.

Taking the heavy set of keys from a hook by the coffee machine, Placido led Santiago out, leaving the Alhambra in Manolo's capable hands. Conchita joined them.

The house, completely empty seemed vast. On three floors it had fourteen rooms altogether, not including the cellars which led out to a large patio and garden on the south side below street level.

Santiago was not only impressed, he was flattered to have been asked to do the job, he was full of unexpectedly good ideas and started from the top.

The attic, which Placido had not even considered, could be converted into a little flat for Maria when she got married. Two rooms, a kitchen and a bathroom, The third floor, three rooms with a central bathroom the second floor the same, the first floor be the clothes shop leaving the ground floor as an extension to the Alhambra Bar.

Another alternative would be to knock passages through to the floors above the Alhambra, have the whole of their house as the pension and restaurant and most of the house as their private residence with the shop.

Or again, they could move the bar into the Velasco-Torres house...

'I will have to think *hombre*,' Placido interrupted. So many new ideas had suddenly been suggested that he felt quite numb. 'We'll have to discuss all this with Maria.'

'How is Maria?' Santiago asked, unexpectedly.

'*Muy bien, Muy bien.*'

Was Santago another suitor? Was Maria the belle of the pueblo every young man was after? Did Santiago have more than the family's interest at heart when he suggested converting the attic?

To have Guardino as Maria's father-in-law was out of the question. Besides, with the *pensión*, with all those beautiful rooms to offer tourists, Don Anselmo's boys might come and stay, for long periods at a time.

The next day Placido took Don Anselmo round the Velasco-Torres house and he was even more full of ideas.

First, the Alhambra should not be changed at all. It had been successful all these years, an *ambiente* had been created which worked, on no account should it be altered. A door, leading from next door to the bar would be enough, otherwise nothing.

In the hotel, however, there should be a quite beautiful entrance hall, not big, yet large enough to have comfortable sofas and nice carpets and a small reception desk. A good painting or two on the walls and a few antiques. The stairs should lead up from the hallway in a gentle curve. A glass door should lead straight into Maria's boutique.

'Hotel? Boutique! You are talking as though this were Madrid, Señor.' Placido pointed out.

'Think big, Placido. Think big. Though I am the last one to want to attract tourists to this pueblo, I know, and you know, that it is inevitable, therefore let us do the thing property and have the right man in charge of the right place with the right atmosphere from the start.'

Placido was flattered.

Don Anselmo went on as they climbed to the first floor. 'This *piso* should have two rooms, two suites in fact, large rooms with double beds and sofas. I'm not suggesting you should install televisions as in the Marbella hotels, but the rooms should be airy. The type of visitor you should attract will be the aesthetic traveller, the adventurer who will try to relive the lives of bygone days when the rich discovered India and the Far East from the comfort of luxurious hotel bedrooms.'

Placido was beginning to feel unsettled. Don Anselmo, it seemed was getting carried away.

'On the second floor,' the doctor went on as they climbed the further flight. 'Well, here you could have four rooms. You should also install a bidet in each room. People may use them or not but a bidet allows them to contemplate the fact that they are in a civilised hotel.'

On the third floor Don Anselmo hesitated. He looked out of the window with the southern aspect and gauged the height of the ceilings, then saying nothing he went further up to the attic and gasped. The attic had no partitions, no walls, it was just one large area with dusty wooden floorboards and small windows overlooking the valley.

'You must rent this to an artist. You should leave this exactly as it is and rent one room on the third floor and this to an artist. I know the very man.'

And, becoming more and more enthusiastic, he paced the attic, measured the height of the walls, paced it again, and examined the slope of the roof.

'You will have to put in a skylight.'

'A skylight?' Placido repeated. 'Looking south?'

'No *hombre*, looking north, here not this side. Artists work by the northern light, it is softer, yet stronger.'

He was learning. With Don Anselmo in the village he was learning.

'I will rent it from next month for a year, for him,' Don Anselmo said. 'Agreed?'

'To what?'

'To rent me this studio.'

'Studio?'

'Of course *hombre*. This is an ideal studio.'

'It gets very hot.'

'Artists are always cold. They are poor and hungry and therefore do not mind the heat. Twenty-five thousand pesetas to include the cost of the skylight and the use of the third-floor lavatory.'

Placido did not hesitate.

'Who is this artist?' He asked.

'You will meet him in due course. He is very quiet, very shy, but he is a very great artist.'

And Don Anselmo led the way down to the third floor and went into a small room to throw open the shutters which looked eastwards towards the back of the village.

He stood there quite a time looking at the roofs of the other houses, the olive oil factory below, the electric pylon which had been stuck there spoiling the view of El Cierro.

Placido wondered what fascinated this learned man so much.

'That's Asuncion and Bartolomoeo's house isn't it?' he asked pointing.

'Yes,' Placido said surprised that the doctor should know where Asunscion lived. 'But they're not there any more, they left with El Lobo.'

'Did they?'

'It was rumoured that he came into an unexpected sum of money, and begged them to go and live with him in Granada.

'Good for him.'

Don Anselmo gazed at the house for a little longer, then said. 'And no one knows what happened to El Lobo's sister?'

'It was said she got killed. Paquito, El Lobo's uncle disappeared as well.'

And as Don Anselmo was closing the shutters on the view, perhaps because of a trick of the light, Placido suddenly saw him as a very young man, as though he was seeing a ghost. An association of ideas, no doubt, but for a second Don Anselmo looked like the young Paquito. Then when the doctor went into the hallway and started down the stairs, Placido again noticed a resemblance, a movement; Don Anselmo was remarkably like Paquito who had saved El Lobo's sister from her brother's madness, so many years ago.

'Paquito?' Placido said softly, just to satisfy himself.

And Don Anselmo instinctively turned around.

'It *is* you? It is really you?'

And Don Alselmo smiled a sad smile.

'Yes, it is me.'

'But why? Why hide? Why change your name?'

And Don Anselmo sat down on the stairs and patted the place next to him for Placido to join him.

'When I first came back here I expected people to remember me, but then I realised that I had changed so much and the village had changed so little that it would be best to remain as an *extranjero*. It was more comfortable. I thought Asuncion might remember me, or El Lobo, but they didn't. And I

114

preferred it that way. It was nice to be here when they sorted themselves out, it was nice to be able to help them, too.'

'You gave El Lobo the money to go to and settle in Granada.'

'Yes. But I didn't want anyone to know of this. I changed my identity so long ago, Paquito was short for Franciso, it wasn't a comfortable name during the war for a man who was anti-Francisco Franco, so I changed it to Anselmo, and with a new name I lived a new life. I had studied medicine in the Jelar hospital, did not join either side but volunteered to help the Red Cross. After the war I was kept on in a Madrid hospital, studied very hard, passed all my exams and was successful. Now all I want to do is retire here, near my own village where I was born.'

Placido could hardly believe his ears! Don Anselmo was Paquito. One of them. Not an *extranjero* but one of them!

'All we need now,' he said 'is for Gonzales to come back and the village will be compete!'

And as though he had powers of premonition, Conchita's voice rang up the stairwell from below.

'Placido are you there?'

'Yes?'

'Guess who's back?'

'Gonzales? Both Placido and Don Anselmo shouted in unison.

'How did you know?'

'We didn't *mujer,* we didn't'

And they both started down the stairs.

'You won't tell anyone will you. It is important to me,' the doctor said.

'I won't tell anyone señor,' Placido said. 'I swear it on my daughter's head.'

And they went out into the street and round to the bar Alhambra's entrance.

Gonzales was standing there smoking a large cigar. He wore an impeccable white suit, silk shirt, silk tie, white socks and had two heavy gold rings on his fingers.

He had arrived in a taxi and quite obviously was in no way trying to hide the fact that he was rich.

After greeting Placido warmly and shaking hands with Don Anselmo, he ordered everyone who was in the bar a drink.

'Communism is dead,' he declared outloud. 'Only a Capitalist society can work!'

No one took any notice because some time ago everyone had decided he was mad. Furthermore, they had decided that the village did not need a mayor, let alone Gonzales.

'I have a serious and sad announcement to make Gonzales went on. 'I am leaving you!'

No one reacted.

It was not world-shattering news, no one actually cared. But he didn't notice.

'I am leaving you because I have got married! And I have got married to one of the most beautiful and wealthiest ladies in the land!'

Placido nearly choked as he drank his coffee. Together with Conchita and Don Anselmo, he had sent this lunatic on a wild goose chase but he had found and married her?

'Vincenta Turena de Lara Baron?' Placido asked incredulously.

'No *hombre*, her daughter! Doña Vincenta married a French industrialist who died leaving her everything to their one child, a daughter. When I got to Valadolid, because of a love letter I received, I only found the daughter staying there, trying to sell the house. She was astounded that her mother should have written to me, but then realised why and fell in love with me herself. So we got married!'

'And Doña Vincenta?'

'Well after that of course she denied every having written such a letter. She lives in France.'

'How old is your bride? Don Anselmo asked.

'Eighteen,' Gonzales said with a big grin.

And for a moment Placido thought he saw a trace of envy in the Doctor's eyes. Well, why not? What man would not envy another's eighteen year old wife, if she were pretty?

And he went back to his chores behind the bar and reflected that, over all, taking everything into consideration, on the whole he had managed his life pretty well and had nothing to envy anyone. Indeed, he had managed everybody's life pretty well. Gonzales, Don Anselmo, El Lobo, Teresita, Eloisa, Esteban, even the film people.

In fact, it could be said that the true Maestro of Almijara was not that fat father of twins, Miguel Muñoz, but himself!

GLOSSARY

ALCALDE	Mayor
ANÍS SECO / DULCE	Dry / sweet anis
AYUNTAMIENTO	Town hall
BODA	Wedding
CALLEJÓN	Alley
CAMPO	Fields, countryside
CULOS	Bums
DUEÑO	Landlord
ESCRITURA	Deeds
EXTRANJERO	Foreigner
FAENA	Display, performance of the bullfighter
FANFARRÓN	Blusterer, windbag
FELICIDADES	Congratulations, good wishes
FONTANERO	Plumber
FRAMBUESA	Raspberry
HIJAS MÍAS	My daughters
LO SIENTO	Feel sorry
MAJO	Elegant, good looking, but slightly arrogant
MANZANILLA	Camomile
NIÑOS DE PAPA	Spoilt brats
NO IMPORTA	Doesn't matter, never mind
NOTARIO	Notary
PENSIÓN	Small hotel
PROPINA	Tip
QUÉ PASA?	What's the matter? What's up? What's happening?
QUÉ TAL?	How are you?
QUÉ VA!	No way! (expression)
SALA DE ESTAR	Living room
TAPAS	Snack
TIENDAS	Shops
TONTO / A	Silly fool, idiot
VEN	Come here (command)

Drew Launay, Maribel and the *Alhora* books

Drew Launay   *Maria Isabel Martin Rodriguez*

I didn't exactly have to lock her up in the flat or tie her down to the bed when my wife Isabel discovered that she was expecting a baby, but she was a tiresomely restless mother-to-be, until l hit on the idea that she could help me with the novel I was writing about village life in Spain.

Lying on the sofa, out poured anecdote after anecdote about the inhabitants of the various pueblos she had lived in when her father had been a travelling doctor around the Granada province. I sat close by and typed out the stories, linked them to the characters in my novel, turning fiction into near fact.

When the first book was finished, titled *The Olive Groves of Alhora,* the publishers suggested that marketing it under Maribel's full name would be hugely beneficial. So as soon as the baby was born, a little blonde girl, off went my wife on a promotion tour of the British Isles, appearing at book fairs, giving lectures at Women's Institutes on the glories of Spanish life, signing her autograph on hundred of copies, while I changed the nappies and sterilized the feeding bottles.

The book became so successful that I wrote a sequel, *The Maestro of Alhora.*

When I decided to republish them in 2006 I changed the name of the main village to Almijara, and hence the books' titles, primarily as a tribute to the area where the books were written, in the foothills of the Sierra de Almijara mountains, but also in recognition of it as the place where I have spent so many happy years.